8 Bodies is Enough

STEPHANIE BOND

DEDICATION

To the readers who keep the Body Movers series alive—thank you.

CHAPTER 1

"LADIES AND GENTLEMEN, the travel time from Atlanta, Georgia, to Las Vegas, Nevada, is approximately four hours, thirty minutes. We should arrive around 7:00 p.m., local time. Please sit back and enjoy the flight."

Carlotta Wren distantly registered the flight attendant's effervescent voice. For the past few days leading up to her trip to Vegas with Peter Ashford, her mind had been running on a loop, stubbornly replaying her last conversation with Jack Terry. She'd called to tell him she had news about where her fugitive parents had been hiding, but he had preempted her report with a personal declaration.

Liz Fischer is pregnant.

I've known for a while, Jack. But good news—Wes isn't the father after all.

I know…because I'm the father.

She had disconnected the call. On the heels of acknowledging to herself she loved Jack, the announcement had been especially hurtful, slamming a door on the future she had imagined with him. Their last night together was still fresh in her mind—she could still feel his hands on her body. And hadn't he nearly professed his love for her then, too?

For all she knew, he'd whispered the same words to Liz when they'd been procreating.

"You're thinking about him, aren't you?" Peter asked, breaking into her thoughts.

Carlotta startled guiltily, then turned her head toward her

companion. "Hm?"

"You're thinking about Randolph, aren't you?"

"Um…yes." The other man who'd been taking up space in her head lately—her father.

Peter clasped her hand. "Don't worry. He's not going anywhere this time—the feds will see to that."

Indeed, Randolph was cooling his heels in the federal penitentiary in Atlanta after appearing out of nowhere to save her from a madman and being taken into custody by Jack.

Except she'd finally figured out he hadn't appeared out of thin air, but from the long-empty house where she and Wesley had grown up and where Randolph had been monitoring a listening device he'd apparently placed in the wall of their townhome before he'd skipped town.

"Forget about your parents for a few days," Peter said. "Let's try to have fun."

She conjured up a smile, fighting the shame rising in her chest. Peter had no idea she had an ulterior motive for suggesting the trip. In the thirty-second encounter she'd had with her father when she and Hannah had wormed their way into the federal pen in disguise and she'd asked about her mother, he'd told her she'd find what she was looking for at "home." And among his things in her childhood home where he'd been hiding out, she'd found a receipt for a post office box in Las Vegas. The real estate agent she'd contacted about the house had recently sold it to a Bill and Melanie Randolph. She'd only dealt with the husband but the wife was supposed to be joining him. When pressed for an address, the agent had become suspicious, would only confirm it was a post office box in Las Vegas.

So if Carlotta had put together the puzzle pieces correctly, Valerie was somewhere in Vegas waiting for word from Randolph to rejoin him in Atlanta. When she hadn't heard from him, it would've taken a simple Google search to learn he'd been arrested and incarcerated. She was probably trying to figure out her next move.

Carlotta prayed she found her mother before she relocated. Randolph had also said he'd stashed evidence to exonerate himself, but he couldn't come forward yet. She'd gone over the expansive Buckhead house systematically, but had found nothing of interest other than the receipt. Not knowing what she was looking for was a huge handicap, but it stood to reason he'd left the evidence in a safer place—with Valerie? Hannah had helped her conduct hundreds of dollars' worth of paid people-searches online, but they'd yielded no Vegas address for a Bill or William or Melanie Randolph.

The post office box was all she had to go on.

"When is Wes coming out?" Peter asked.

"I'm not sure—he had to clear it with his probation officer and his boss at the city IT department. It's nice of you to let him use the extra room that came with the package."

"Happy to. So he's still doing community service?"

"Yes," she murmured. She made a mental note to ask Wes if he was close to fulfilling his sentence for hacking into the city courthouse records. That incident seemed so long ago—and paled in comparison to some of Wes's antics since.

"And he's still working for the morgue?"

"Occasionally. Coop hasn't called him as much lately."

Peter made a derisive noise. "At least Cooper Craft isn't calling *you* to go on those ghastly body moving runs."

"Someone has to do it, Peter."

"Well, it doesn't have to be you," he said, then lifted her hand for a kiss. "You have your job at Neiman's—and now your boss is talking about a promotion when you get back. I'm proud of you."

"Thank you." After a wedding expo, a famous designer had made comments about wooing her away from the department store. She suspected the interest had spurred her boss Lindy into action. She conceded it felt good to be wanted.

"Wesley should be in college," Peter remarked.

"I know," she said, hating the defensive note in her voice. Instead, the boy genius was performing community service, moving bodies, and working undercover for the APD in a loan shark organization. "Maybe when things are resolved with Dad's case, Wes will settle down."

Peter nodded and started to say something, then pulled his hand over his mouth.

"What?" she asked.

He sighed. "There's something I have to tell you."

For a few hysterical seconds, she thought Peter might tell her *he* was the father of Liz's baby. Even more crazy was the thought of how happy that would make her. "Whatever it is, just tell me."

"I'll have to work some when we get to Vegas. Apparently, Walt was supposed to meet with clients in the area before he fell ill."

Walt Tully was a partner in the investment firm Mashburn & Tully where Peter worked and her father had once been a partner.

"James Brody asked me to step in since I was coming out anyway."

Carlotta tempered her reaction—she would need some time on her own to search for her mother, so Peter's impromptu assignment was a gift. "What will you have to do?"

"Just goodwill lunches and drinks." He looked contrite. "With Randolph being back in the news, the partners are doubling-down on customer relations, just to reassure everyone the firm is solid."

"I understand," she said, trying to hide her relief. "Don't worry—I'll find something for me and Wes to do."

She hadn't told Wes about talking to Randolph in the pen, finding his hideout, or the clue leading her to Vegas. She justified her decision with the fact that since she told him they were going to Vegas, she'd seen Wes scant minutes here and there, and she worried if she told him about the post office box in Vegas, he'd tag along even if his probation office and boss both said no. Right now, she needed for him to stay out of trouble.

Especially after the baby-daddy scare with his attorney, Liz.

Plus she didn't entirely trust Wes to keep family secrets from the blond barracuda. That said, her brother deserved to know what was going on, so if he got to Vegas, she was going to sit him down and tell him everything.

"I hope you have a plan to keep him away from the poker tables," Peter said.

"I don't have to. He's not twenty-one, so no casino is going to let him gamble. Besides, he doesn't have enough money to get into trouble."

"That never stopped Wes before," he said mildly.

"I know. But he swore to me he wouldn't borrow more money from those loan sharks and on that subject, I believe him."

Wes seemed to have been scared straight, although she didn't want to know those harrowing details. The undercover job—that she wasn't supposed to know about—served two purposes: ingratiating him to the APD and paying off his debt to The Carver.

Hopefully that obligation would also be met soon.

"What's going on with his girlfriend?" Peter asked.

"I'm not sure. There was a, um, *hiccup*, and he hasn't mentioned Meg lately." Peter didn't know about the Liz-Wes-Jack paternity mix-up, and she was loath to tell him because she didn't want to hear him say I-told-you-so where Jack was concerned.

But he'd told her so.

"Too bad about Wes's girlfriend." Peter moved his head closer to hers. "I was hoping he'd bring her so we'd have plenty of alone time."

"We'll have our own room," she said with a little laugh.

"I know," he said, this voice thick with meaning. "And it'll be nice to be away from all the distractions in Atlanta."

He meant Jack, of course. And Coop. And Randolph.

And Peter had his own distractions. The few times they had tried unsuccessfully to reignite their physical relationship, it had taken place in the home and the bed he'd shared with his deceased wife in a marriage fraught with tension.

She and Peter both had baggage, ghosts, and issues galore.

But Peter Ashford had been persistent and patient while she'd tried to sort through her feelings for him and Jack and Coop. And while the other two men had always been there when she needed them and provided tempting diversions on occasion, Peter was the only one who had professed his feelings and offered her a future.

Indeed, their trip was compliments of a package he'd won in a charity auction a few months ago. They were sitting in first class and she was lightly buzzed on wine and warm nuts they'd been served while everyone in coach was still searching for a place to stuff their carry-on. A first-class life was what she had to look forward to if she would only open her heart to him.

Carlotta looked into Peter's earnest blue eyes and nodded in assurance. "I think this might be just what we need to get things on track."

He smiled, then grimaced into a yawn. "I'm sorry," he said behind his hand. "With Walt out of the office, I've been working long hours."

She nodded in sympathy. Walt Tully had been hospitalized from an overdose of prescription drugs just as his former partner and fugitive Randolph Wren had been captured. So in a sense, she and her family were loosely responsible for Peter's exhaustion.

"Why don't you take a nap? I'll wake you before we land."

"If you're sure." But he was already reclining his seat, and as the plane went airborne, he was softly snoring.

When they reached cruising altitude, Carlotta asked a flight attendant for a blanket to tuck around Peter's sleeping form. Even in slumber, his features, hair, and clothing were neat and polished, so different from—

No, she wouldn't think of Jack. She reached down to the inexpensive pink beaded elastic bracelet she'd bought, pulled it up and let it snap against the sensitive skin of her wrist. The zing of pain made her flinch. A good reminder that *Jack equals pain.* If she zapped herself every time she thought of him, eventually her body would get the message.

She hoped.

Fatigue pulled at her, too, but her mind wouldn't shut down. She passed the flight watching a couple of movies—one a romantic comedy featuring two people who were impossibly ill-suited overcoming all their differences to find happily ever after, and the other a con she and her gal pal Hannah could've pulled off with more panache.

Throughout, her mind kept wandering to what awaited her in Vegas. Would she find her mother? Would Valerie be happy to see her? Would she and Peter finally turn a corner?

Below them the colored lights of Vegas came into view, twinkling with promise. The city looked magical and Carlotta was inexplicably shot through with the wondrous sense that here, anything was possible.

Plus ten points.

CHAPTER 2

"WELCOME TO THE VIP SUITE, Mr. and Mrs. Ashford."

Carlotta opened her mouth to correct the uniformed bellman.

"Thank you," Peter said, clearly pleased at the assumption. Then he gave her a wink.

She swallowed her irritation—Peter was only trying to protect her honor.

Besides, it was hard to be cross standing in the middle of such opulence. The massive room was enveloped in gold and white carpet, curtains, and upholstered furniture, with subtle touches of black here and there.

The bellman swept his arm toward the enormous bed, swathed in miles of luxe fabric. "The California king mattress can be adjusted for firmness and massage." He was tactful enough not to point out the mirrored tiles on the ceiling, but she blushed under Peter's heated glance.

The man walked past the bed into a wide hallway and indicated the tall wood doors on either side. "His and her walk-in closets, each with a dressing table and a safe for your valuables."

Beyond the closets, he threw open double doors to reveal a breathtaking white marble bathroom with gold fixtures. "Two showers, each fitted with dual shower heads and steam. The floor is heated. The tub is equipped with fifty jets." He pointed. "Use this panel for a light show. Use this panel for the sound system. The television here and in the sitting room receive over two hundred channels, and you can place bets using the special remote."

8

He led them back into the living area. "Of course, the bar is fully stocked, and room service is available twenty-four seven. We have six restaurants, an exercise facility on the tenth floor, and pools on the fifth, fifteenth, and twentieth floors. Is there anything I can get for you before I leave?"

"We're good," Peter assured him, folding a bill into the man's hand.

He gave a curt nod of thanks and left. Carlotta looked at Peter and lifted her hands. "Was this the best you could do?"

He laughed and pulled her close. "I take it you approve of the accommodations?"

"Yes. Are you sure the auction package is covering this?"

"Well, since I have to work while I'm here, I decided to get a room upgrade. Plus I'm trying to impress you."

"Mission accomplished," she murmured, lifting her mouth to receive a very good kiss.

"Well, that's not the only mission," he whispered.

Her pulse drummed higher as she returned a second, more hungry kiss. She and Peter had been each other's first lovers, and they had once been electric together. She wanted them to get to that place again.

He lifted his head. "I'm starving—are you?"

She blinked. "Uh—sure, I could eat."

"Why don't we unpack and freshen up, then grab a quick bite and come back and...relax?"

"Okay." She reasoned Peter was probably a little nervous, too. Which was understandable considering the ups and downs of their relationship.

Carlotta took her time unpacking, thinking she hadn't brought enough clothes to do justice to the expansive walk-in closet with padded hangers, teak shoe shelves, and velvet-lined drawers. On display, her travel wardrobe looked a little blah, but she'd purposely packed neutral clothes so she wouldn't be particularly noticeable or memorable as she searched for her mother. She

STEPHANIE BOND

guiltily stowed a red wig and a blond wig in the custom drawers, along with a couple of floppy hats.

Still, not everything she'd packed was practical. From tissue paper, Carlotta removed two sets of exquisite lingerie she'd brought for the occasion, one blue and one yellow, Peter's favorite colors on her. After she tucked away the bits of silk, she snapped the pink bracelet on her wrist—twice.

The built-in safe was the size of an armoire. Out of curiosity she opened the heavy steel door to find a yawning space inside. But considering the furs, jewelry, cash, and designer accessories most guests who booked this type of room traveled with, she supposed it made sense. And while the Chanel clutch and the Fendi sandals she'd brought were pricey, they weren't exactly safe-worthy.

She showered quickly and changed into a short black skirt and taupe silk blouse, wound her hair into a low French twist, then found Peter in the sitting area, parked in a club chair.

He didn't hear her approach on the thick carpet, so she was able to study him unobserved. By anyone's standards, Peter was a handsome man—tall and fit, with aristocratic features and impeccable grooming. But at the moment, his chiseled mouth was pinched into a line and his forehead creased with worry. Carlotta's steps faltered—was she to blame for his tense expression, or was Peter worried about something else?

He glanced up and his face rearranged into a smile as he stood. "You look beautiful, Carly."

"Thank you. You look nice, too. Everything okay?"

He smiled. "Never better."

The hotel lobby was abuzz with activity, but as soon as they walked outside they were immersed in the full teeth-jarring spectacle of Vegas. Carlotta's senses were assailed by blaring noise, blazing lights, and a barrage of motion. The crush of bodies was overwhelming. Flamboyant street entertainers vied for attention amid the cacophony of ringing slot machines and jackpot bells from children's games. The smells of cooking food blasted them from all directions. The range of people milling around them was mind-boggling: young, old, older...male, female, unisex...cowboys, sheiks, showgirls.

They found a Japanese seafood restaurant overlooking an outdoor plaza and ordered a sushi platter to share. When the sumptuous rolls were set in front of them, Carlotta's mouth watered. No way would Jack eat sushi—

Under the table, she snapped her elastic bracelet.

"What do you think of Vegas so far?" Peter asked, using chopsticks like a pro.

"It's...shiny," she said, watching a jester juggle jumbo sparklers for a gathering crowd. "I see the appeal. It looks like everyone here is happy."

"That's probably true when people arrive," he said, polishing off a morsel. "Unfortunately, some people leave a lot worse off."

Thinking of the task ahead of her, Carlotta chewed slowly, hoping his words weren't prophetic. Recalling how worried he'd looked when she walked upon him at the hotel, she angled her head. "Is something bothering you, Peter?"

"No. I don't mean to be a downer, but in my line of work, I can't tell you how many times I've fielded a call from a client saying they lost a bundle of their retirement fund at the craps table."

"Yikes."

"On the other hand," he said, nodding to a bride and groom strolling along the courtyard below them in white gown and black tux, "some people come to Vegas to change their life."

Carlotta smiled at the glowing couple, but something she'd detected in Peter's voice made her look back to him.

He was holding a red ring box containing a familiar Cartier ring. It was the ring he'd first given her when they were young. After her father's scandal had broken and Peter had ended their engagement, she had kept the ring for years, pining for him, until she'd been forced to sell it to a pawn shop. By that time Peter was back in her life and had hunted down the ring, then upped the ante by adding a large glittering diamond on either side of the center solitaire. Since then he'd been trying to convince her to wear it.

"Do you remember our agreement?" he asked.

Her throat was tight, so she nodded. When Randolph had returned unexpectedly, she'd suggested to Peter they spend some time apart so their relationship wouldn't be a conflict of interest for him at work. He had agreed, but only if she promised to use the separation to consider wearing his ring.

"So, now that you've had time to think about us...will you wear my ring, Carly?"

Her heart flapped around in her chest. How could she not be dazzled by the amazing piece of jewelry? And flattered that Peter had created it solely for her? But she wanted to know what meaning would be attached to it, what he would expect of her.

"What are you asking, Peter?"

"This isn't exactly the way I'd planned to do this, but..." He slid out of his chair and down on one knee. "Carlotta Wren, will you marry me and make me the happiest man alive?"

Gasps sounded around them and she realized they were garnering a lot of attention from other diners.

"Say yes!" a woman shouted, setting off a chorus of encouragement from all around the room, including the servers.

"Say yes! Say yes! Say yes!"

Carlotta swallowed hard as a hot flush crept up her face. Her pulse raced and she was having trouble breathing. Peter looked so handsome and so hopeful. He would love her and give her a good life. They could be happy—if only she would stop punishing him for a youthful mistake. Besides, how did the classic song go?

If you can't be with the one you love...

"Yes," she said on an exhale.

Peter whooped with pleasure as he removed the ring to slide onto her finger. The restaurant erupted in applause. He pulled her into his arms and kissed her heartily. Peter's happiness was contagious, and her chest welled with deep affection for him and all they'd been through. She laughed and waved to the people sitting around them, thanking them. As the cheers subsided, she and Peter reclaimed their seats. Her stomach rolled from all the excitement, and her palms were moist. She stared at the ring, its many carats sparkling under the lights.

"It's awesome," their waitress said, her voice wistful. "And a step up from that plastic bracelet, for sure."

Carlotta frowned.

"But I wouldn't be showing it off, if you know what I mean." As the woman turned away, she jerked her head toward another table.

Carlotta glanced over to see a pair of questionable-looking men fixated on her ring and exchanging knowing looks.

"Right," Peter added quietly. "Vegas is riddled with pickpockets and thieves. As soon as we get back to the room, we'll store it in one of the safes."

"Okay."

"By the way, I wasn't going to say anything about the bracelet, but it doesn't seem like something you'd wear. Is it sentimental?"

"Not really," she hedged, covering the cheap pink beads with her hand. "It's...to remind me of something. It's...not important."

He grinned wide. "So we're engaged."

"Again," she added without thinking. When his smile faded a bit, she said, "I'm sorry. This is a new beginning."

"A new beginning," he agreed, his eyes darkening with desire. "Let's get out of here."

While Peter paid the bill, Carlotta snapped a picture of the ring on her finger and texted it to Hannah.

Ten seconds later, Hannah texted back. *Is that what I think it is?*

Yes.

Fuck. I knew I should've gone to Vegas with you.

I didn't invite you.

Friends don't let friends get engaged on the rebound.

Carlotta frowned at the screen.

"Something wrong?" Peter asked.

"No," Carlotta said, stowing the phone. "I was just sharing the good news with Hannah."

"I know Hannah doesn't like me."

"She doesn't know you."

"It's okay," he said. "Goth Girl and I have nothing in common—except you." He dropped a kiss on her nose. "Ready?"

Carlotta nodded, biting back a smile. Little did Peter know, Goth Girl was the heir to HAL Properties, a holding company for exclusive hotels. Carlotta had caught Hannah red-handed in designer duds and airbrushed makeup looking downright gorgeous at a business event. Peter would probably change his mind about Hannah if he knew...which disappointed her a little. And she wasn't ready to tell him Hannah's family was one of Randolph's clients who lost big when he was accused of fraud over a decade earlier.

She was still grappling with that news herself.

On the walk back to the hotel, Peter clasped her left hand and smiled every time she caught his glance. But she could tell his body language was tense, and she wondered if he was worried about being intimate with her. Things in that department had nowhere to go but up—literally. But hopefully their new status as a couple would be the catalyst they needed in the bedroom.

When they turned a corner, Carlotta looked back and stiffened.

"Is something wrong?" Peter asked.

She continued walking at a slightly faster pace. "Those men from the restaurant are following us."

"Where?"

"Don't look back."

"I'm calling 9-1-1," Peter said, his head pivoting. "Where's a taxi when you need one?"

"Quick, in here," she said, pulling him into a souvenir shop.

"But they'll catch up to us."

"They won't know it's us." She walked down the aisles, picking up packages as she went. Without breaking stride, she carried the items to the nearest checkout counter. A bewildered Peter paid while she opened the packages.

"Is there a back door?" she asked the guy at the register.

He pointed. "Through the stock room, but once you go out, you can't get back in."

"Fine," she said, already heading that way. She handed a wrinkled white paper jumpsuit and plastic wig to Peter. "Put these on."

"But—"

"Hurry."

She pulled a cheap white dress over her head and situated a cottony wig over her dark hair. They'd gone in the front door Carlotta and Peter, and when they went out the back door, they were Marilyn and Elvis.

"This way," she said, when they exited onto a side street. "We'll get behind them. How's 9-1-1 coming?"

"Still on hold," Peter said, exasperated.

They turned right and right again, then merged with foot traffic on the main thoroughfare.

"There they are up ahead," Peter said, squeezing her hand. "They're looking for us."

"Keep your phone up to hide your face. Be casual."

A few minutes later, they walked right by the men who were craning and scanning the crowd. Fifteen minutes later, they walked into their hotel lobby.

"Hello?" Peter said into the phone. "Thanks, but never mind." He ended the call and made a disgusted noise. "What if our lives had been in danger?"

"But they weren't," Carlotta said, threading through the bank of slot machines meant to snag guests who had just arrived. Then she laughed at the picture Peter presented—an outraged imitation Elvis. "Look at you."

He grinned. "Look at you! That was fun. Wait—where did you learn to do that?"

"I improvised," she said breezily, stabbing the elevator call button.

But he was looking at her sideways. "I'm not sure I believe you."

"Newly engaged and you're already doubting me," she chided as the elevator doors opened.

He walked on behind her and picked up her beringed hand. "Newly engaged," he repeated. "That sounds amazing. I love you so much."

"I love you, too," she murmured.

While Peter pushed the button for their floor, she snapped the elastic bracelet against her wrist.

As they approached their room, she breathed deeply to calm her nerves. She could tell Peter was nervous, too, from the way his hand shook slightly when he used the key card to open the door. When they walked inside, the room seemed smaller and the bed seemed larger. The cover had been turned down in invitation. Their gazes met...

Carlotta wet her lips.

"Why don't we get out of these costumes?" he suggested.

Undressing each other sounded sexy to her, but when she took a step toward him, he walked past her.

"I'll meet you back out here?"

"Oh...okay."

"Do you want me to put your ring in the safe in my closet?"

"I'll put it in the one in mine," she said, trying not to feel deflated.

"Let me know if you need a hand."

Carlotta frowned after him. She could think of lots of things for his hands to do. She snapped the bracelet on her wrist—hard—then retrieved the red ring box from her bag and went to her walk-in closet. Things would be better between her and Peter once they'd made love. The comforting thought made her quicken her pace.

She tugged on the door of the safe, then realized she'd inadvertently closed the door when she was looking in it before. Since she hadn't changed the combination, though, the door opened when she pulled up on the handle. Carlotta jumped back when a large object came rolling out. A few seconds passed before she registered the large object was a man's body dressed in the hotel's uniform. She screamed.

"Carly?"

"Peter—come quick!"

Peter burst into the closet. "What the hell?"

"He was in the safe."

"Is he *dead*?"

"Yes. He's cold."

"You touched him? I'm calling security. Come out of there, Carly. I don't want you involved."

Too late. Because the dead man's face was familiar—it was Johnson, the guy renting the house next door to her and Wes's townhome in Atlanta.

The guy she'd suspected of watching them.

Minus ten. Minus ten. Minus ten.

While Peter was on the phone shouting at hotel security, Carlotta retrieved her phone and reluctantly placed a call of her own.

On the fourth ring, Jack Terry's groggy voice came on the line. "Carlotta? Do you know what time it is?"

She realized it was way late on the East Coast. "Tell Liz I'm sorry to disturb her beauty sleep."

"It's not like that. I'm not… Where are you?"

"In Vegas. And I'm in trouble."

"You're supposed to get in trouble in Vegas. It's Vegas."

"There's a dead man in my room."

He sighed. "Of course there is. Okay, I'm awake. Talk to me."

CHAPTER 3

THE BLACK TOWN CAR CIRCLED the parking lot before coming to a stop by the curb. The driver-side window buzzed down, revealing a big, dour face.

"This had better be good, Little Man, to call me on a Sunday."

Wesley Wren loped over, feeling light and happy for a change. "It is, Mouse. Here." He handed The Carver's collection guy a brown paper bag.

Mouse looked wary. "What's this?"

"See for yourself."

Mouse opened the bag and peeked inside, then glanced back up. "What the hell?"

"You've never seen cash before?"

"Don't be a smartass."

"That's enough to clear my debt with The Carver, and a little extra for goodwill. Feel free to skim some off the top for yourself."

Mouse frowned.

"Not that you skim off the top of collections," Wes added hastily.

Mouse crunched the bag closed. "What'd you do, rob a bank?"

Wes smiled, reliving the discovery of a bag of cash in the wall of the townhouse in the course of doing repairs. It had taken him a while to count it, but all told, it was more than five hundred thousand dollars. He suspected his father had put it there before he went on the run ten years ago, with the thought of returning for it, or leaving it for his kids to live on in their parents' absence. But if Randolph had left instructions on where to find the money, they'd gotten waylaid.

Although it had occurred to Wes the instructions might be in the Christmas packages under the tree in the living room he had refused to let Carlotta open. If so, *damn.*

Or maybe Randolph had simply forgotten about the money. If he'd absconded with as much money as he'd been accused of stealing from Mashburn & Tully, five hundred grand would've been a mere oversight.

But it could've made a big difference to his life and Carlotta's over the past ten years. How many times had he seen his sister cry over late bills and failing appliances they couldn't afford to replace? Plus she could've gone to college.

Both of them could have.

It's why he didn't feel guilty about spending some of it now to get himself out of a jam, and why he had a tidy sum sewn into the lining of his jacket for his trip.

A snapping sound brought him out of his reverie. Mouse was scowling. "Bank robbery is federal. You don't mess with that shit."

Wes stabbed at his glasses. "Relax, I didn't rob a bank. I just got lucky is all."

"Won the lottery, huh?"

"Something like that. Gotta run—I have to catch a flight."

"Where you headed?"

"Vegas."

"You don't say?"

"Yeah. My sister and her boyfriend are out there on vacation and invited me to come out. I'm taking a friend."

"A lady friend?"

"No, my buddy Chance. He loves Vegas."

Mouse nodded toward the passenger seat. "Get in, I'll give you a ride to the airport."

"I was planning to take the train."

"No, really. Get in."

Wes knew better than to argue. But his feet were heavy as he walked around to climb into the front seat. "Thanks."

"Nice day for a drive," Mouse said casually, pulling away from the curb and easing out of the parking lot into traffic. The big man maintained a stoic silence until they merged onto the connector leading south to the airport and put a few miles behind them. "The boss is going to be happy you paid off your debt, but with this much money, he's going to ask questions."

"Tell him I won it in a poker game."

"Were you playing with someone from the Treasury Department? Those are brand new bills."

Wes swallowed hard and decided not to answer.

"Or maybe it's reward money from the D.A.'s office for snitching?"

Wes jerked his head around. "What? No!"

"So you haven't been talking about our headless friend who wound up in the morgue?"

If he lived to be a hundred, he'd never forget pulling the teeth out of the decapitated head and leaving it in a field for the birds. "You never told me the guy's name, remember?"

"But you could've tagged me for being involved."

"I didn't, Mouse. I wouldn't snitch on you."

"You don't have to. I didn't off the guy."

Wes gaped. "You didn't?"

"Nah, it was one of Dillon's guys."

"Someone who worked for The Carver's son? Was it Leonard?" Leonard was the muscle head his probation officer was engaged to.

Mouse looked surprised. "You know Leonard?"

"No." Wes held up a hand. "Forget I said anything. I don't want to know." He already felt guilty about not telling E. Jones her boyfriend was bad news.

"So the cops *have* been leaning on you."

Wes was relieved to see the sign for the airport exit. "They can lean all they want—I'm not talking."

Mouse sighed. "The problem is, it looks bad—you cashing out like this, then skipping town."

"The money didn't come from the cops, and I'm not skipping town."

Mouse smiled. "I knew you wouldn't run out on your baby, not after what your daddy did to you."

Wes chewed on his lip, then grunted. "Turns out, the baby's not mine."

"No shit? Aw. Is that good?"

"Mostly," Wes admitted.

"Bet Meg is happy about that."

Meg Vincent and her sweet strawberry mouth were done with him. "Actually, she couldn't care less. Go to the south terminal."

Mouse took the turn. "So you don't have a reason to stay here."

Wes looked over. "My sister is here, and my dad, remember? The feds are still holding him in the pen."

"No offense, but I got the feeling your dad doesn't want anything to do with you."

Hurt and anger fused in Wes's chest. It was true Randolph hadn't initiated the paperwork necessary to allow Carlotta and Wes to visit him. And when someone Mouse knew inside the pen had tried to communicate with Randolph on Wes's behalf, his father had refused.

Wes waved toward the ticketing entrance. "You can let me out here." He was opening the door before the car came to a stop. "Thanks, man."

"Wes?"

Reluctantly, Wes turned back. "Yeah?"

Mouse splayed one big hand. "I guess this is goodbye. If your debt's paid, you don't need to do collections anymore."

He hadn't thought about that. "I guess you're right." He reached into his backpack and pulled out the cell phone Mouse had given him for exclusive communication between them. "I won't be needing this."

Mouse shrugged. "Keep it. I might call you sometime to say hello."

That was crap, but it was a nice gesture. "Okay."

"Good luck, Little Man."

"Thanks. You, too, Mouse."

He closed the car door and stepped back, then with mixed emotions, watched the Town Car pull away. Mouse had been like a mentor to him, had helped him get clean and given him advice. He would miss the big lug. Some.

Wes turned and strode into the airport, whistling under his breath to feign composure as he approached security. He ran a hand over the back of his moist neck. In hindsight, it might not have been the best idea to sew twenty-five grand into the lining of a jacket when the temps were still warm. But it was too late to change plans now.

It wasn't illegal to carry a chunk of cash on a domestic flight, but if it was discovered, he'd probably have to answer some questions. Being on probation and using a suspended driver's license as a picture ID might be enough to have him detained. He'd read online the x-rays could detect a stack of organic matter, i.e., paper money, so he'd spread it out. If he was lucky, he'd look like the average college student traveling to Vegas for a little fun and breeze right through.

"Hello, Wesley."

Wes looked up to see Jack Terry standing nearby with a duffel bag. He swallowed a foul word. "Hey, Detective. Didn't take you for a jet-setter."

"Yeah, well, duty calls. Where are you headed?"

"Vegas."

Jack gave a little laugh. "Me, too. Carlotta didn't mention

you were coming out."

Wes squinted. "You know she's out there with Peter, right?"

"Yep."

"You two planning to roll the dice to see who gets Carlotta?"

Jack's mouth tightened. "No. A dead man turned up in her hotel room."

"Ah. The two of you figured out a way to off Peter altogether?"

Jack wasn't amused. "I guess you haven't talked to your sister?"

"Not since she left. I was trying to give the lovebirds some privacy." He enjoyed seeing the vein bulge in Jack's neck.

"Carlotta opened her room safe and a guy rolled out."

Wes might've been surprised except they were talking about Carlotta. "Bummer. And Vegas doesn't have police officers?"

"The dead guy is the man who was renting the house next to yours."

Wes felt his jaw go slack. "The photographer?"

"Yeah, he said his name was Johnson?"

"I only met him once." Wes's neck burned as he remembered convincing himself their parents had been hiding out next door all these years. He'd dragged Carlotta over there to ring the doorbell and instead of their mother answering the door, some half-dressed Abercrombie-looking guy said they'd gotten him out of bed.

"Carlotta seemed spooked by the guy," Jack said. "She made me listen to their conversation once when he came to the door."

"What did he want?"

"To return a vase…and he asked her out."

Wes snorted. "Just another lovesick guy obsessed with Carlotta, following her around and trying to get in her pants."

"Mind if I join this party?"

Wes turned his head to see Cooper Craft walking up wearing a fedora and a black messenger bag. "And here's another one."

Coop looked confused. "Come again?"

"So Carlotta crooks her finger from the other side of the country and you two come running?"

Coop smiled. "Personally, I'm going to Vegas for the buffets."

"Uh-huh," Wes said.

"Hey, thanks for this," Jack said to Coop and extended his hand for a shake.

"Glad to help, Jack. And it's a good time to squeeze in a little hiking. Things are slow at the morgue."

"That's because Carlotta is out of town," Jack said with a grin. Coop gave a hearty laugh.

Wes shook his head. "Both of you are pathetic."

Coop clapped him on the back. "Come on—we'd better get in the security line if we're going to make this flight."

Wes flinched, wondering if Coop could feel the layers of money.

"Expecting it to be cold in Vegas?" Coop asked, patting the jacket.

"Air conditioning," Wes said, wiping at a bead of sweat dripping down his temple. The movement produced the sound of rustling paper. "I heard they keep it cranked up in the casinos."

Coop surveyed him quizzically, goosing Wes's anxiety. He glanced toward the exit and wondered if he should make a run for it.

"You heard right," Coop said. "But you're not old enough to go near the gambling tables, so you should be fine to lose the jacket once we get there." He let his hand drop. "There are plenty of things to do in Vegas besides gamble.

"Yeah, I heard the Hoover Dam is nice," Wes offered in a blatant attempt to suck up.

"That sounds safe," Coop agreed, giving him a pointed look.

Jack moved forward, and Coop fell in step next to the detective. The two men found the end of the security line, talking between themselves. Wes brought up the rear. Great—he was already worried about getting through security with the money undetected, and now he had an audience. He was tempted to wait for Chance, but his buddy hadn't texted back his whereabouts and for all he knew, Chance could be sitting at the boarding gate.

"Laptops, shoes and jackets in a bin," a TSA guard announced to the crowd. "Belts, too, and empty your pockets."

Wes gingerly removed the jacket, wondering if everyone—including Coop, who was right in front of him removing belt, hat, and shoes—could hear the crackle of paper. He folded the heavy, inflexible jacket and put it in the gray bin, then untied and slipped off his tennis shoes and set them on top. After he emptied his pockets of coins and keys, he waited, feeling vulnerable and guilty standing in his sock feet.

Now he couldn't even run if he needed to.

The line moved quickly and as Coop walked into the body scanner, it was Wes's turn to put his bin and backpack on the conveyor belt.

Even without the jacket, Wes was sweating profusely. He watched his bin go into the luggage scanner, then he stepped into the body scanner and assumed the jumping jack position. He was waved through the scanner. He stepped to the other side and exhaled when he saw his bin come out of the luggage scanner.

Then the conveyor belt stopped and went in reverse, sucking the bin holding his jacket and shoes back inside.

Wes swallowed hard. He calmed himself by reasoning the TSA couldn't confiscate the money—he had a right to have it in his possession. But at this point, trying to explain it to Coop and Jack would be the pisser.

Ahead of him, the two men were putting their belts and shoes back on. Coop looked up and nodded at Wes. Wes nodded back.

His heart was thumping like a bass speaker. He glanced at the agent standing nearby and tried to act casual—and innocent. "Hey," he offered with a little smile.

But the agent remained stony faced.

At the luggage scanner, the agent had waved over two helpers to look at something on the screen. They looked up and one of the agents walked toward him. "Sir, are these your items?"

Shit. "Yeah."

"Do you mind if we take a closer look?"

He debated saying no—he could do that, couldn't he? But probably not without causing a national incident.

"No problem," he said, but his voice came out sounding like he was going through puberty.

The agent grabbed his backpack in one hand and his bin in the other and walked to a table. Coop and Jack had noticed the commotion and were watching—and waiting. Coop narrowed his eyes at Wes. Wes returned a watery smile.

The agent unzipped his backpack and rummaged through it. Wes got a new panic attack wondering if in addition to the cash he was smuggling through, was it possible he'd left something illegal in his backpack? Considering the collections visits he'd made with Mouse, he might've overlooked a shank or a knife blade or a lock pick kit or an ice pick or brass knuckles or...

His stomach bottomed out. What if Chance had put pills or weed in his bag?

He clawed at his itchy, sweaty neck. Coop and Jack knew something was amiss, and were making their way back to him.

Just as the agent found something.

Shit, shit, shit.

The man pulled his hand out of the backpack and held up his contraband.

A can of deodorant body spray.

"Sir, you're not supposed to have aerosol cans in your carry-on. If you want to keep this, you'll have to check your bag."

Wes had to catch himself to keep from falling on the floor in relief. "Nah, you can keep it."

The agent tossed the can into a receptacle full of odd and sundry items, then handed the backpack and the bin to Wes.

"Have a good flight, sir."

"Thanks." He carried his stuff to a nearby bench to re-dress, breathing deeply to help the adrenaline subside.

"Everything okay?" Coop asked.

"You seemed worried back there," Jack added suspiciously.

"Yeah, I was worried," Wes said. "Now I'm going to stink."

"What else is new?" Coop said.

"Nice hat," Wes jabbed back.

Coop touched the brim, unfazed. "Thanks."

"Let's go," Jack said. "The plane boards in ten minutes."

Wes laced up his shoes and shrugged into the money-jacket, then grabbed his backpack and jogged after the men. They took the indoor shuttle to their concourse and made it to the gate at the end of boarding. Wes didn't see Chance and hoped his buddy was already seated on the plane. But when he boarded and slowly made his way to his assigned seat, the one next to his was empty.

Wes sagged. With twenty-five grand to bet, Vegas would be fun, but it would be more fun with Chance along. But Chance was so head over heels for Hannah, he probably couldn't stand the thought of leaving her for a few days.

He couldn't be angry. If Meg would give him the time of day, he might not have come either.

He pulled out his phone and texted Chance. *Dude where RU Plane is leaving*

A few seconds later, a text came back. *Auuuuuuuuuuuukkkkkk*

Which in Chance's case, could mean anything—he could be on the commode, having a stroke, or jerking off.

"Ladies and gentleman, we're ready to close the door and push back, please turn off all electronic devices and fasten your seatbelt."

Wes sighed. Maybe Chance could catch a later flight.

"Wait!"

A passenger bounded through the door and if Wes hadn't recognized the voice, he would've recognized the thud of his buddy's big body coming to a wheezing halt.

"Made it!" Chance crowed triumphantly, and a few passengers cheered.

"Because I pulled you on my suitcase," said his exasperated companion. Pierced and tatted Hannah Kizer was barely winded.

That explained the erratic text. Wes grinned when his buddy made it back to his seat. "That was close, dude."

"Hannah decided to come!"

"He sees me," Hannah snapped. "My seat is back here—wait, is that *Coop*?"

"You and Chance can sit here, and I'll take your seat," Wes offered to Hannah.

"No way," Hannah said, already moving down the aisle. "I'll see you two bozos on the other side."

Wes glanced at Chance to see if his feelings were hurt, but Chance was glowingly oblivious to Hannah's dis.

"This is going to be a fucking blast," Chance said, settling back in his seat. "You're going to love Vegas, man—anything can happen there."

Wes nodded. Maybe it was the money he was wearing next to his skin, but he definitely felt as if he was on the brink of something big happening.

"Ladies and gentlemen," a flight attendant announced, "we're ready to depart. Travel time from Atlanta, Georgia, to Las Vegas, Nevada, is approximately four hours, thirty minutes. We should arrive around 12:00 noon, local time. Please sit back and enjoy the flight."

CHAPTER 4

CARLOTTA SNAPPED the pink beaded bracelet against her wrist. Thank goodness it was waterproof—but *ouch*, it hurt more when the elastic was wet.

She lathered her skin, trying to ignore the sensations triggered by the warm, soapy water and the massaging pulse of the shower head. On top of her and Peter's romantic efforts being interrupted last night, talking to Jack had resurrected so many wrong, no-good thoughts. And she was keenly aware how inappropriate her erotic urges were in the wake of finding Dead Johnson in her safe...but she couldn't turn them off.

Releasing a pent-up groan, she turned the temperature lever deep into blue territory for an icy blast that took her breath away.

A knock on the door sounded. "Everything okay in there?" Peter asked.

She turned off the shower. "Yes. I ran out of hot water."

"Well, you've been in there a long time."

She closed her eyes briefly. Peter was being understandably overprotective after a "stalker" had followed her to Vegas and presumably broken into her room to lie in wait and suffocated for his trouble. With Jack's blessing, she hadn't told Peter or the police she suspected Dead Johnson had moved in next door to her and Wes—and subsequently followed her to Vegas—for a reason other than a perceived romantic attachment. If she were a betting woman, she'd put her money on it having something to do with Randolph's reappearance.

But she needed for Peter to believe the danger was past.

"I was just taking advantage of this amazing bathroom," she called.

After last night's "regrettable mishap," they'd been upgraded from a huge suite to a monstrous suite. She stepped out of the glass shower that would easily accommodate fifty people and glanced around the glittery spa-worthy room, taking in the gilded tub in the center of the room, the gold-leaf mosaic in the tile around the room, the wall of beveled-glass mirrors, and the enormous crystal chandelier that reigned over it all.

And this was *her* bathroom. Peter had his own equally posh lavatory on the other side.

"Wes just called our room—I told him to come up."

"Oh, good. I'll be right out."

She was missing her little brother more than she thought she would. In truth, she missed Atlanta and everyone in her familiar world. She'd been in Vegas for less than twenty-four hours and she was feeling unwelcome, as if the city didn't want her here and would devour her if she stayed too long. She'd hoped to start looking for her mother today, but it would have to wait until tomorrow when Peter would be occupied with clients.

If Wes was here, Jack was probably in town, too, or would be soon. He'd told her he'd check in after he talked to the Vegas police. Just knowing Jack was close by made her feel—

She gave the bracelet a snap.

The matter at hand was putting up a good front for Wes. She'd planned to talk to him about what had led her to Vegas, but if Johnson had followed her hoping she'd lead him to Valerie and/or Randolph's former hiding place, whoever had sent him would probably send a replacement. She couldn't count on Wes to be smart under pressure.

And she couldn't count on Jack not to give her up.

And she couldn't count on Peter not to make her go home.

Damn. In hindsight, she would've been better off to come to Vegas alone...or to bring Hannah.

Then she chided herself—this was supposed to be a chance for her and Peter to have a fresh start. Okay, so the quick marriage proposal had caught her off guard, but it almost felt as if there was no middle ground for her and Peter. Dating on and off had gotten them nowhere, and she suspected Peter needed proof of her forgiveness before he could get back to a confident place, sexually speaking.

Then she sighed—not that they'd gotten there yet. Between the incident, then answering questions from the police, then being moved to another room and the time difference, they'd both been comatose by the time they crawled into bed.

Although Jack wouldn't have let—*snap*!

Carlotta winced, then wrapped her hair in a towel, turban-style, and pulled on a spa robe. She opened the door and stepped into the hallway, walking toward her dressing room. When she heard voices, though, she decided to give Wes a hug before getting dressed.

She had padded into the main room several feet before she realized it wasn't Wes who'd arrived—it was Jack...and Coop. She hadn't expected Coop to come, too, but it made sense Jack would bring someone to examine the body whom he could trust. Carlotta stopped, and they all looked her way.

There they were, the three men in her life. Carlotta flashed back to playing the Mystery Date board game with girlfriends as a pre-teen, opening the little plastic door to different types of men. Peter was dressed in crisp chinos, golf shirt, and loafers. Jack wore jeans, leather jacket, and boots. Coop wore cargo pants, a pullover, and sneakers. All handsome and sexy, each in his own way.

"Look, Carly—Officer Terry and Mr. Craft came all the way out here to investigate your stalker." Peter seemed less than pleased.

"Detective," Jack corrected sourly.

"Doctor," Coop amended good-naturedly.

"You didn't mention you'd called the detective," Peter said lightly.

"I'm sure I did," Carlotta lied.

"Maybe," Peter conceded. "It was rather late by the time we went to bed. Together."

That was subtle. "Hi, Jack…Coop."

"Hi," they chorused.

When she realized they were staring, she remembered what *she* was wearing. The awkward intimacy of the other men being in a room she was sharing with Peter seemed tangible. A flush warmed her face as she pulled the robe tighter. "Sorry—I thought you were Wes. Give me a few minutes to get dressed."

Carlotta fled to her room-sized closet and hastily pulled on a casual jersey sheath. She combed out her long hair and wound it, still wet, into a low knot at the nape of her neck. For makeup, she only took time to apply lip gloss and mascara. After grabbing a cross-body bag and her phone, she pushed her feet into sandals and hurried back to the men, primarily because she was worried what they'd talk about in her absence.

"So," Jack said when she walked up, lifting a glass of dark liquid in her direction, "you and Peter are engaged."

Her smile froze.

"Congratulations," Coop offered congenially. The liquid in his glass was clear—probably club soda in deference to his recovery.

"Thank you," she murmured. "I see Peter shared our good news."

"I did," Peter said, beaming.

"Can I have some of whatever that is," she asked, gesturing to Jack's glass.

"Of course," Peter said, pouring her a drink from a decanter. "It's aged bourbon," he said when he handed it to her. "So you might want to sip it."

Carlotta tossed back a generous mouthful, taking perverse

33

pleasure in the burn down her throat and into her empty stomach. "How was your trip out?"

"Good," Jack said.

"Uneventful," Coop added. "Unlike your trip so far."

She took another drink. "What all did Peter tell you? About the dead man, I mean."

"That you came back to your room after he proposed," Jack said, with the merest lift of an eyebrow.

"And when you opened the safe to put your ring inside," Coop continued, "the body fell out."

"That must be some ring," Jack added mildly.

"It is," Peter confirmed. "In fact, when we left the restaurant, a couple of shady-looking men followed us. I think they intended to rob us." Then he smiled and put an arm around Carlotta's shoulder. "But we outsmarted them."

"Really?" Jack asked, sounding amused. "How's that?"

"We ducked into a costume shop—"

"It doesn't matter," Carlotta cut in with a dismissive wave. "The point is, we lost them."

Peter's phone rang. He pulled it from his belt clip and checked the screen. "Excuse me, I need to take this." He gave her an apologetic look, then moved toward his dressing room as he answered the call.

Carlotta gave Jack and Coop a grateful smile. "Thank you both for coming."

"No problem," Coop said.

Jack looked at Coop. "What was it Wesley said? That when Carlotta crooks her finger, we come running?"

Coop gave a little laugh. "I think that was a joke, Jack."

"The joke is the room you and I got stuck with compared to this one," Jack said, nodding to the view the corner windows afforded. He briefly swung his gaze to the gigantic mussed bed that sat on a raised portion of the room, like a stage, complete with spotlights.

"The hotel gave us an upgrade," she murmured, irritated. Her sleeping accommodations were none of Jack's concern. "So Wes was on the same flight?"

"And his roommate," Coop said.

Carlotta made a face. "Chance came, too?"

"And Hannah."

She grinned. "Hannah is here?"

"She's back to that Goth getup," Jack said.

"Yeah, what happened to Uptown Hannah?" Coop asked.

"You might not want to mention her other, um, *persona*," Carlotta said. "She doesn't want Chance to know. They're kind of...dating."

Coop's eyebrows rose. "Hannah is dating Wes's chubby roommate?"

"I know," Carlotta said. "There's no accounting for taste."

"You said it," Jack remarked in a way that made her think he was talking about her and Peter.

"Speaking of congratulations," Carlotta said to Coop. "Did Jack tell you he's going to be a father?"

Coop blinked his eyes wide. "What?" He looked at Jack. "That's huge. Who—I mean...wow."

Jack's smile was tight. "Liz Fischer."

"Oh?" Coop extended his hand. "That's great, man."

Jack accepted his handshake. "Thanks."

But Carlotta regretted saying anything—it wasn't her news to share, and it sounded spiteful. And hadn't Jack come all this way to help her? "Jack—"

"Let's get this show on the road," Jack said, then drained his glass. "I talked to the local police and they gave me copies of their files, but I want to take a look at the crime scene myself. Mind if I use your room phone to call hotel security to meet us there?"

He was already moving toward a phone on the wall next to the bar, so she didn't respond. She set down her unfinished drink and pushed it away, feeling contrite.

Coop gave her a little smile. "Last night had to be quite a scare." He caught himself. "Finding the body, I mean."

"Yes." She cast about for a way to relieve the tension that shrouded the fussy room. "I wonder what happened to Wes. Peter said he was on his way up."

"That's my fault," Coop said. "I saw an Atari arcade and showed him how to play some of the classic games. When I left he was still going."

"That sounds harmless enough."

"Is he staying out of trouble?"

"Barely," Carlotta said. But she'd take that. Heaven knew she didn't need any more trouble this week.

CHAPTER 5

WES PLAYED THE VIDEO GAME for a few minutes more after Coop walked away. When he was sure Coop wasn't coming back, he sent a text, then turned and strolled through the lobby and out the door, past the fountains and the terraced flower garden, past the flamingo pond and a giant stone sculpture of a tiger, to the taxi drop-off area marked with international flags. As instructed, he stood in front of the flagpole flying the Switzerland flag.

He people-watched to pass the time. Vegas definitely attracted an oddball assortment of residents and visitors. It was almost as if everyone who didn't fit in anywhere else on the planet, came here to fit in with other misfits.

Present company included, he thought wryly.

Taxis were running nonstop, depositing wave after wave of people returning from the dinner hour. A muscle head wearing a skullcap emerging from a cab caused Wes to do a double-take. From a distance, the guy looked like Leonard, his probation officer's boyfriend. Then he shook it off—Leonard was on his mind because of his conversation with Mouse yesterday about who'd offed the headless guy in the morgue.

Unbeknownst to the luscious redhead E. Jones, Leonard ran drugs between the Carver's son Dillon and Chance, and Wes was sure the steroid-riddled thug had once robbed a poker den at gunpoint, depriving Wes of a sizable pot he'd won. But was the guy capable of such a grisly murder?

A burgundy van pulled up next to Wes and braked abruptly. The passenger side window zoomed down.

The driver was bald and skinny, with poppy eyes. "Wesley?"

"Yeah."

"Get in."

When he hesitated, the van started to pull away.

"Wait!" He opened the door and swung up into the seat before the van was moving again.

"I'm Nick," the driver said, wrangling the large steering wheel. The area behind the front seats was an organized office, with built-in cabinets and computer equipment. A heavy-set guy with glasses sat behind a desk typing on a keyboard.

"Chance said you need an ID?" Nick asked, pulling into traffic.

"Yeah. One good enough to pass muster in the casino."

"That's all we do, man. You got the cash?"

"Three hundred, like you told my buddy."

"With that baby face, it'll be five."

Like he had a choice. "Okay."

He'd had the forethought to transfer ten of the two hundred fifty Franklins from the Velcro'd lining of his jacket to his wallet. He pulled out five of the bills and handed them to Nick, reveling in the heady feeling. Money was power—he understood why his dad had gone into investment banking.

Nick used a thin piece of wood to push the bills into the slot of a padlocked metal box that was bolted to the floor, then jerked his thumb toward the back. "Mister will take care of everything. Go on back."

Wes duck-walked into the rear of the swaying van and sat where Mister pointed, in front of a screen. Two printers the size of washing machines took up a good portion of the floor space. The cabinets were stocked with plastic cards, seals, and various inked stamps. This was a high-tech operation.

"Did you bring your real driver's license?"

Wes removed the card from his wallet and handed it over.

"Atlanta, Georgia. I suggest a driver's license from a southern state to go with your accent. How about Alabama?"

"That works," Wes said.

The guy tapped a few keys, and a template for an Alabama driver's license appeared on one of the flat screens. He started typing in Wes's name.

"Shouldn't I use a fake name?"

"It's up to you, but it's better to use your own name in case someone asks to see a credit card or something else with your name on it to corroborate your ID."

Wes pursed his mouth and nodded.

"Age." The guy looked at him over top of his glasses. "I wouldn't go more than twenty-six."

"Okay."

"Give me a street address you can remember, but doesn't belong to anyone you know."

He could remember something relating to Meg. "Sixty-nine Vincent Street."

The guy frowned. "Sixty-nine is the most commonly used street number on fake ID's. Give me another number you can remember, Casanova."

"Thirty-six." Meg's bra size.

"Thirty-six Vincent Street. What town? Should be a real town in Alabama, smaller is better."

"Ozark."

"Ozark, Alabama," Mister said, typing and nodding. "Not bad." He pulled out a drawer full of folded T-shirts in all colors and designs. "Take off your jacket and put on one of these shirts."

"Why?" Wes asked, panicked.

"It's really better if you're wearing something different in your ID picture than what you're wearing when you present it."

"Oh." They'd thought of everything. He slipped off the jacket and pulled a plain brown T-shirt over the gray Skrillex T-shirt he wore.

Mister pointed. "Look into that camera and give me an

expression like you've been standing at the DMV all afternoon."

He heard a click.

"Okay, now sign your name on this digital pad."

Wes did.

"Take off the T-shirt, and sit tight for ten."

"You're sure this will fool the casino?" Wes asked.

"If you get banned from a casino," Mister said, "it's something you did, not me."

Fascinated, Wes watched as the man created the fake driver's license layer by layer. He'd prided himself on creating authentic-looking fake tickets back when Carlotta was party-crashing, but this was hardcore. When the license came out of the printer, Wes couldn't believe it. "It looks perfect."

"Which you don't want," Mister said. "The issue date is over a year ago, so we need to make this look like a year-old driver's license." He dropped it on the dirty black floor of the van and stepped on it a couple of times, ran a piece of sandpaper over the edges, then used a curling iron to put a bend in it like Wes's real driver's license.

"That way it looks like it's been in your wallet. By the way, always keep your fake ID in your wallet—flags go up when people pull their ID out of a pocket. It's too convenient. And keep your real driver's license in a separate place so you don't accidentally flash both licenses."

"Got it," Wes said, feeling a rush of adrenaline.

"Also, this is important—you can't use it for twenty-four hours."

Wes's shoulders fell. "Twenty-four hours?"

"It's the smell," Mister said. "The heated plastic has a distinctive odor that's a dead giveaway to the bouncers, but it wears off in twenty-four hours. Do not try to use it before then, capiche?"

"Yeah," Wes groused.

Mister handed over the fake license like the gift it was.

"You're all set. You can go back up front."

"Thanks, man." Wes awkwardly made his way back to the front seat just as Nick was pulling the van to a stop at the same place where he'd picked Wes up. They had been moving the entire transaction.

"So long," Nick said. "Tell Chance thanks for the referral."

"Will do." Wes opened the door, climbed out, and closed the door behind him. The van wasted no time in pulling away.

Wes turned to walk back toward the hotel entrance with a spring in his step. Even faced with a twenty-four-hour ban, the excitement of being in a poker game began to bubble in his chest. His hands itched for cards to hold. He'd been waiting for this—the chance to sit in a real Vegas poker game, with real money to back him up.

He stopped so abruptly, he got a headache. He pulled his hand down his Skrillex T-shirt as a blinding realization hit him. He'd left his jacket in the van—and all the money.

Wes spun around, sick with panic. Now what?

As he stood there trying to decide whether to shit his pants or puke on the sidewalk, the burgundy van reappeared next to him. "Forget something?" Nick called.

His jacket came flying out the window, landing on his head. By the time he clawed his way to daylight, the van was gone again. He frantically examined the jacket lining—still intact, ditto for the cash. Despite the heat, he put it on, weak with relief.

That was close.

CHAPTER 6

"WES SEEMED ON EDGE at the airport."

Carlotta pulled her gaze from Jack, who was phoning hotel security to meet them at the crime scene, back to Coop, who was sipping on his club soda.

"I'm not surprised," she said. "It's one of the reasons I invited him to come with us. He's been through a lot lately. And he's upset because Randolph hasn't let us visit him in jail. I thought a change of scenery would help."

"So you still haven't talked to your dad?"

The brief conversation they'd had when she and Hannah had infiltrated the prison didn't really count, but she hedged with a shake of her head. "We still don't have an explanation of why my parents left, or what happened to our mother."

"I'm sorry. You must be going a little crazy. And now this stalker situation, too."

"It doesn't help," she agreed. "But enough about me—how are things at the morgue?"

He shrugged. "Same. We're supposed to get a new chief M.E. soon."

"And how is Rainie?" Rainie Stephens was a pretty reporter for the *Atlanta Journal-Constitution* Coop sometimes kept company with.

"Rainie's good," Coop said with a smile. "Rainie's always good. She's...easy."

As opposed to always being mired in drama, Carlotta thought dryly. Touché.

Jack hung up the phone and motioned toward the door. "They'll meet us at the room."

Carlotta went around the corner to let Peter know. He had stepped into his dressing room to take the phone call, and his back was to her.

"—she hasn't talked to Randolph."

Carlotta stepped back, out of sight, her ears piqued.

"To my knowledge, the son hasn't talked to him either."

Her heart pounded. Who was Peter talking to? And why was he reporting back on her and Wes?

Peter grunted. "The plan is to be here all week. Do whatever you have to do."

She blinked—what did that mean?

"I need to hang up," Peter said. "I'll call you if there are any updates."

She backtracked quietly, then tossed, "Let me tell Peter" over her shoulder as if she was just going to fetch him. When she stepped to the door of the dressing room, Peter turned with a smile, his hand over the phone's mike. He must've made another call.

"Who are you talking to?" she asked pleasantly.

"Oh...it's the office."

"On Sunday?"

"Everyone is working overtime to get ready for an audit," he said in a rush. "Do you need something?"

"We're going to do a walk-through of the other room," she said, sounding amazingly normal. "I'll be back in a few minutes."

"Should I go, too?"

"No need," she assured him. "It's routine."

"When you get back, we'll go do something fun, just the two of us," he promised.

"Sounds good." She smiled, then turned and headed back to where Jack and Coop were waiting.

Carlotta put her hand over her mouth to suppress nauseating fear. Flashing dots danced before her eyes. She'd been right to withhold information from Peter about talking to her father and why she wanted to go to Vegas.

"Everything okay?" Coop asked.

Carlotta looked up to see him standing near the open door, waiting. Gratitude welled in her chest. She nodded, flustered. "That's what I get for drinking whiskey on an empty stomach."

Coop reached into his pocket and withdrew a protein bar. "Knock yourself out."

"Thanks." She blinked back sudden tears.

"Hey, something *is* wrong."

She pulled back her shoulders as she peeled open the snack. "No...it's just what you said earlier about Rainie—that she's 'easy.' That sounds so nice."

He winked as she walked through the door. "I don't believe you'd be satisfied with easy. I think you tried that once."

He was referring to their brush with romance—she deserved that. Instead of responding, she took a bite of the protein bar and looked around the empty hallway. "Where's Jack?"

"He went ahead."

Jack had been eager to put some space between them, she presumed. And if Jack was going to have a family, she needed to get used to lots of space between them.

As she munched on the snack, she felt Coop's inquiring gaze trained on her, but thankfully, the crowded elevator car prevented further conversation as they rode to the appropriate floor. When they alighted, she led Coop down a hallway to the room she and Peter had first checked into. On the door was a sign announcing the room had been decommissioned and no admittance.

Coop knocked, and the door was opened by the head of hotel security. He recognized Carlotta from the previous night and waved them inside.

The gold and white suite was rendered a little less spectacular by the addition of black and yellow crime-scene tape. Coop followed her through the bedroom and down a hallway toward the walk-in closet where Jack was inspecting the safe and comparing it to notes from a file folder.

"Hey," he said in acknowledgment. "Carlotta, do you want to fill in the blanks?"

"Where do you want me to start?"

"What time did you check into this room?"

"Around 7:45 p.m. I looked in the safe when I unpacked around eight, and it was empty."

"Did you put anything inside?"

"No."

"Was there anywhere else he could've been hiding?"

"Sure. We didn't look in every closet, or under the bed."

Jack's mouth twitched down. "Then what?"

"Then Peter and I went to dinner, and when we came back, I came in to put the ring in the safe. I opened the door and the man fell out."

"What time was that?"

"About ten o'clock, just before I called you."

"Was the safe door locked?"

"No, just closed. I hadn't reset the combination, so I pulled up on the handle and it opened."

"And you could tell the man was already deceased?" Coop asked.

"Yes. He was cold."

"It looked to you as if he'd suffocated?"

"It certainly looked that way."

"Yet there's a door release lever inside that's hard to miss...and it appears to be working."

"And there were no marks on his hands to indicate he'd tried to get out," she added.

Jack raised his eyebrows.

"I checked," she murmured.

"So maybe someone killed him earlier and put him in the safe?" Jack mused aloud. "We won't know the time of death until we get the results of the autopsy."

"I checked his eyelids," Carlotta offered, "and there was no rigor, so he'd definitely been dead for less than two hours."

The men stared at her, then Jack looked to Coop for confirmation. He nodded.

Jack scowled, then made notes on the sheet he was reading. "I hate to denigrate fellow police officers, but this documentation is slipshod. And the pictures are terrible—all eight of them."

"Do they have a name yet?" Carlotta asked.

"No," Jack said. "The hotel says he wasn't employed here, which we already suspected. He told you he was renting the house next to yours, so I have someone looking into the owners. For now all we have to go on is the name he gave to you and Wes— Johnson."

"Have they run his prints?" Coop asked.

"There's a wrinkle," Jack said.

"He had no fingerprints," Carlotta supplied. "They were as smooth as a baby's bottom."

The simile had just slipped out, but Jack gave her a sardonic look. "You checked his fingers?"

"Yes."

"Do I want to know what else you checked?"

"There was no blood, and no tears or holes in his clothes that would indicate a wound."

Jack sighed. "Anything else?"

"He had a small tattoo at his waistline. I noticed it the day Wes and I met him."

"Oh?" Coop asked with a sly smile.

"His shirt was open," she said pointedly. "It looks military to me." She pulled out her phone, found an image, then showed the screen to Jack and Coop.

Jack sputtered. "You took pictures of the body?"

"Of course. And the crime scene. Do you want them?"

His mouth tightened. "How many did you take?"

46

She consulted her phone. "One hundred sixty-three. I can put them in your Dropbox."

Jack slow blinked. "Come again?"

"Send them to me," Coop said. "I'll make sure Jack gets them."

"Do you want the videos, too?"

"Videos?" Jack parroted.

"I shot a video before the police arrived, and another one of them investigating the scene. The last one is a rather large file, let's see—almost ninety minutes long."

Jack's face turned purplish. "The local police let you shoot a video of them while they were working?"

"Of course not." She pointed. "I set my camera on that shelf behind my shoes. They didn't even know it was on."

Coop snorted with laughter.

Jack cut his eyes toward Coop. "Don't encourage her."

Carlotta scowled. "You just said the police's documentation was lame. Do you want my files or not?"

Jack jerked his head in concession, then said, "C'mon, Coop. Let's head to the morgue."

"Can I go?" Carlotta asked.

"No," they both said in unison.

She frowned. "You don't have to be rude."

Jack pulled his hand down his face. "Coop, do me a favor and ask the hotel security guy if we can take a look at the footage of their surveillance cameras?"

"Sure, Jack," Coop said, then walked away, out of earshot.

Jack surveyed her with unreadable bloodshot eyes until she squirmed.

"Do you want to yell at me again?" she asked.

"No," he said, sounding exhausted. "I want you to tell me why this guy would follow you to Vegas."

She shrugged. "I don't know."

"Why do you *think* he followed you?"

"You overheard him say he wanted to take me out."

"As irresistible as you are, Carlotta, I can't see the guy trailing you and your fiancé out here to try to change your mind."

"Was that a compliment?"

"Don't go off point. The way I see it, this guy followed you because he thought you could lead him to something he wanted, something to do with Randolph."

She put on her best clueless face. "I don't know what that could be. Randolph won't even agree to let me or Wes visit him. Why would this guy think I knew something?"

"Maybe he thought it was suspicious you would just up and go to Vegas?"

"Then he didn't do his homework. Peter won this trip at a charity auction a while ago. We were headed to Vegas the day I stopped by the townhouse and Abramson attacked me. We had to postpone then, so here we are."

"So there's no special reason for this trip?"

"My and Peter's engagement isn't special enough?"

He studied her face for long seconds, then nodded. "If you say so. But I'm not asking just for your sake—I have explicit orders from my captain to stay away from your father's case. I'm not kidding, Carlotta. My job is on the line."

"Well, I wouldn't want to be responsible for you being unemployed," she said lightly, "seeing as how you're going to have a new mouth to feed."

Jack looked away, then back. "C'mon, we'll walk you back to your room."

They were a quiet trio as they made their way back to the upgraded suite. Carlotta mulled Jack's probing questions about Dead Johnson—if he was following her in the hopes she'd lead him to Randolph's hiding place and to Valerie, who would've hired him? Someone from the D.A.'s office? Mashburn & Tully? One of Randolph's victims?

And what were the circumstances around Dead Johnson's

untimely death?

And if she didn't have enough on her mind, there was Peter's conversation she'd overheard—someone at Mashburn & Tully was paranoid about Randolph talking to his children…but why?

Peter's promise they would do something fun this afternoon, just the two of them, echoed in her head as she approached the room's door with Jack and Coop.

"How long are you both planning to stay in Vegas?" Carlotta asked, inserting the keycard.

Jack shrugged. "I'd like to stay until we get an ID on the body."

Coop nodded. "Hopefully his DNA will be in the system."

"Keep me posted?" she asked.

"Yep," Jack said, without making eye contact.

"Send me those files," Coop said as he and Jack walked away.

She pushed open the door to the sound of voices. On the other side of the suite, Wes, Hannah, and Chance were sprawled on the elegant, pale furniture and apparently working their way through the assortment of food and drinks in the bar. Empty wrappers were strewn everywhere and something purple had been spilled on one of the couch pillows. Peter stood nearby looking irritated and helpless.

"Hey, Sis," Wes called, saluting with a bottle of soda. "This is one hell of a room."

"Our room isn't nearly this nice," Chance said, licking chocolate from his fingers. "We'll probably hang out here most of the time."

Peter's face blanched, but Carlotta welcomed the raucous interlopers.

Hannah pushed up from a chair, holding a bottle of wine by the neck. "What the fuck? Wes said some stalker followed you out here and fucking died in your safe?"

"Hi, yourself. And that's about the sum of it."

"How do you die in a safe?"

"I'll tell you about it later."

"Tell me about it now," Hannah said, steering her away from the others. Then she leaned in close and whispered, "Why the fuck did you get engaged to Peter? I thought you came out here to find you-know-who, not to fuck up your life."

"Can we dial down the 'f' word?"

"Can you give me a fucking answer?"

"Why do people normally get engaged?" Carlotta hedged. "I love him."

"It's me you're talking to. You find out Jack knocked up Liz and suddenly you love Peter?"

"Okay. I *want* to love Peter, and I think I can get there."

"I think I'm going to be sick all over this silk carpet."

"Did you come all the way out here just to give me a hard time about Peter?"

Hannah frowned. "No. In fact, I need your help. I promised my father I'd meet with some VIP piece-of-shit royalty at one of our hotels out here, just to kiss his noble ass."

"So what's the problem?"

"So I can't go looking like this, and I don't want Chance to see me looking like *that*. Can you help me pull this off?"

Carlotta looked past Hannah's shoulder to take in the motley Atlanta crew assembled in Vegas. Had everyone brought secrets with them?

"Sure. Actually, I could use your help, too."

"No problem." Hannah took a swig from the bottle of wine. "So where's the big-ass diamond ring and what's up with the pink Barbie bracelet?"

CHAPTER 7

"THANKS FOR LETTING ME get dressed in your room," Hannah said, fastening her seatbelt.

"Are you kidding?" Carlotta clicked her own belt into place. "I wouldn't have missed seeing the look on Peter's face when you came out." Her friend had gone into the bathroom looking like trouble, and came out looking like the cover of a magazine.

Hannah grinned. "It did feel good to render Richie Rich speechless."

"I think I saw a spark of attraction there," Carlotta teased.

"Oh, no—don't try to pawn your fiancé off on me."

"I'm not."

"I think you are." Hannah gave her a pointed look. "How's the sex going?"

Carlotta sighed. "It isn't...yet."

"Carlotta! This is the time in your relationship when you should be going at each other like rabbits."

"Like you and Chance?"

"Bad example, but yeah. We've had sex seven times since we got to Vegas—and that's while sharing a room with Wes."

Carlotta lifted her hand. "I don't want to hear anymore. You have to admit finding a dead guy in the room is a libido killer."

"Speak for yourself."

Carlotta laughed, shaking her head.

"What's the address for the P.O. box place?"

Carlotta read it off while Hannah punched it into the car's GPS.

"Looks like it's only about eight miles off the Strip, but in this traffic," Hannah said, maneuvering the car onto the jam-packed street, "it'll probably take us twenty minutes to get there."

Carlotta checked the side mirror. "Keep an eye out for a tail."

"You still think Dead Johnson wasn't working alone?"

"I don't know. But if he wasn't, and he accidentally suffocated or had a heart attack in that safe, it makes sense someone would take his place."

"And you think these people believe you'll lead them to your mother?"

"To Valerie, or maybe to the evidence Randolph said he had that would exonerate him." Which could exist only in her father's imagination.

"Who would care enough to follow you?"

Carlotta counted on her fingers. "D.A. Kelvin Lucas, the GBI, the FBI, someone at Mashburn & Tully, one of the people Randolph ripped off—and that's just from the top of my head. Plus who knows what he's been into the past ten years? There could be a whole pile of people looking for Randolph I wouldn't even know about." She pulled a red wig from a bag and used the visor mirror to adjust it.

Hannah turned to look at her. "Are you sure you're okay to do this alone?"

"I can't confide in Peter...yet."

"Why not?"

The phone conversation she overheard kept coming back to her. "I don't trust him not to interfere. And I can't tell Wes yet—I can't trust him not to go off half-cocked."

"But you trust Wes in a casino?"

"He's not old enough to gamble."

Hannah barked out a laugh. "You don't really think that's going to stop him, do you?"

"He told me he's going to watch the poker tournaments to pick up pointers."

"Okay, believe that if you want to."

"I want to. Besides, I offered him a hundred dollars spending money, and he turned it down, said he wouldn't be needing any— so there."

"So, to review, you don't trust the two people you should trust more than anyone else?"

The truth hurt. "The only person who knows everything is you," Carlotta said. The unspoken words hung in the air. The woman who'd withheld until recently the information that her own family had been a victim of Randolph's scams. "If something were to happen to me—"

"Nothing's going to happen to you."

"—you have to tell Wes everything. Promise me."

Hannah's eyes grew serious. "You know you can count on me."

Carlotta nodded. "Yes, I do."

Then Hannah quirked a smile. "Wow, today could be the day you're reunited with your mother. Are you ready for that?"

"I really don't know. I guess I'm afraid to get my hopes up. I'm following a trail of pretty cryptic clues." And if by some miracle she did locate Valerie, what kind of reception would she get?

"What do you know about this post office box?"

"From what I could tell on my phone, it's one of those shipping stores where you can rent a P.O. box."

"Want to do a drive-by before I let you off?"

"Do you have time before your meeting?"

"The dickhead prince I'm meeting will probably think more of me if I'm late." Hannah drove the nondescript rental car around and through agonizingly slow traffic for long minutes. "Do you see anything suspicious?"

Carlotta was keeping an eye on the side mirror. "No. I think we're good."

"Okay, so the place should be a couple blocks down on the

right. This isn't the best part of town."

Carlotta was thinking the same thing. The main drags of Las Vegas were clean and in good repair, but this side pocket was litter strewn and graffiti tagged. And the people hanging out on the corners weren't passing out handbills.

As they drove closer, her heart was pounding. But if she thought Valerie Wren would be standing in front of the business, she was mistaken. It was a sad little storefront with faded window displays, not yet open for the day.

"Where should I let you out?" Hannah asked.

"Drive a couple blocks away, and I'll walk back. It doesn't open for another thirty minutes."

Hannah did as she asked, letting her off outside a coffee shop.

"Thanks, and I hope your meeting goes well."

"Yeah, what the fuck ever. Call me if something exciting happens on your end."

"Okay. If you don't hear from me, I'll see you back at the hotel." Carlotta extended a keycard. "Here's an extra key to my and Peter's room so you can change back. Just knock first, okay?"

"Why? It's not like I'll be interrupting you two having sex."

"Bye," Carlotta said pointedly, then shoved the car door closed.

After glancing around to make sure no cars stood out to her, she casually made her way into the bustling coffee shop where she bought a large latte and a postcard to send to June Moody, friend and proprietor of Moody's cigar bar in Atlanta. She found a pen in the bottom of her bag and jotted a quick note.

Thinking of you. Carlotta

Carlotta sighed. June wasn't the only person she'd been thinking about. She snapped the bracelet a couple of times to keep those dead-end thoughts at bay. *Jack equals pain.*

Her phone vibrated and she checked it, hoping for some word from Jack or Coop regarding the identity of Dead Johnson. Instead it was a text from Peter.

Sorry to be spending the day with clients. I hope you and Hannah have fun.

As far as he knew, Carlotta was going shopping with Hannah. He hadn't questioned her friend's transformation, had just chalked it up to Hannah's oddball personality. But the fact that he'd mentioned Hannah at all meant he was warming up to her. Carlotta pushed down the thought that he was a hypocrite. Everyone who'd seen the new Hannah had responded positively to her new look—except Hannah.

Carlotta texted back *I hope you have a nice day, too.* Then she made sure her phone's location was disabled. Her phone was on Peter's account which, now that she thought about it, might be on Mashburn & Tully's account.

Carlotta brought her fist to her mouth. Had Peter or the company been tracking her whereabouts all along to see if she went to talk to her father in prison? Thank goodness the time she and Hannah conned their way inside the federal pen, they hadn't taken their cell phones.

Then she gave herself a mental shake—she was being paranoid.

Two men walked into the coffee shop and with a start she realized they were the two guys from the restaurant who had followed her and Peter after noticing her ring. In front of them, she spotted their quarry—a middle-aged couple standing in line were arguing, oblivious their clothing and accessories stamped them as novice tourists. The man's zippered backpack was hanging open, exposing a pricey tablet device—easy pickings for a thief.

Knowing the men wouldn't recognize her in the red wig, Carlotta straightened and walked toward them, elbowing her way between the two couples. "Excuse me, not cutting line, just trying to get to the ladies' room. Oh, sir—your backpack is open."

The man and woman stopped long enough to thank her, then began arguing about whose fault it was the backpack was unzipped. Carlotta didn't look at the would-be thieves, just kept moving toward the restroom. Once inside, she closed and locked the narrow door behind her. After checking her appearance in the smoky mirror, she sipped her coffee while reading some of the hundreds of messages that had been scribbled on the yellowing plaster walls in everything from ink to lipstick.

Mark and Jenna, celebrating 12 years!

Metallica rules.

Call Babs 555-5890 to talk or ?

Just be happy.

Doug F. Mitchell is an mf liar! He cheats too.

Carlotta smiled at peoples' urges to leave a bit of themselves in a place so random. If she were going to add a bit of wisdom to the wall, what would it be?

She bit down on her lip. If she wrote the name of the man she thought she should marry, no one would ever know. She pulled the pen from her bag, pressed the tip against the wall in a tiny blank space, and wrote his name in curly cursive letters, as if she were writing in her high school notebook.

Carlotta angled her head, smiling at her secret message to the universe, then something written just below caught her eye.

Valerie W was here.

Her breath caught in her throat. There were probably thousands of Valerie W's in the world, and hundreds who had passed through Las Vegas. But one thing she'd forgotten until this moment was how her mother signed her name and added wings to the "W."

Just like this signature.

Her own message forgotten, Carlotta pulled out her phone to zoom in and take a picture of the signature. Her hand was shaking so badly, the camera lens had a hard time focusing. She ran her finger over the scrawl, as if she could absorb some kind of truth from it, or determine how old it was. Had her mother written it in a bout of loneliness after being ripped from everything she'd known?

She glanced around the small dingy bathroom, imagining her vivacious mother standing here, feeling desperate enough to write her name on the wall. Goose bumps rose on her arms.

The door handle jostled, then a knock sounded. "Hey, there's a line out here."

Carlotta stowed her phone, then unlocked the door and walked out, undeniably rattled.

The two thieves had left—no doubt with a couple of lifted wallets. On the sidewalk outside the coffee shop, she checked the security of her own bag, then headed back to the shipping store. She breathed deeply to steady her emotions, but it was hard not to feel hopeful she might be close to unlocking the secret to her parents' disappearance.

As she approached the storefront, she sipped her lukewarm coffee and tried to act casual. The windows of the business were studded with hand-lettered signs proclaiming "NO Loitering—This Means You." "NO F*cking Smoking." (Which only reminded her how much she craved a cigarette.) And more menacingly "Customers Come & Go at Your Own Risk."

She pulled open the heavy glass door and walked inside, glad to see the man at the counter had a customer. It gave her time to get the lay of the land.

The place was grubby and stale-smelling, with a few missing ceiling tiles. The one-room shop was deep and narrow, with shipping supplies and a counter on the right, and a bank of mailboxes on the left and back walls. She had memorized the post office box number from the receipt she'd found in her father's things: 610.

A quick scan of the numbers led her to the box in question located against the back wall, second row from the bottom. It was one of the smaller boxes, about six by twelves inches. Which was encouraging—a smaller box would likely be checked more often, she reasoned. As the customer at the counter completed his transaction, she casually reached into her bag and pulled out her keyring. She fumbled and jangled the keys, then grunted loudly and said, "Oh, no."

The man behind the counter apparently heard her distress call. "Can I help you?"

She turned and sighed. "I'm a dope. My father is sick and asked me to pick up his mail, but I must've brought the wrong keys. Can you save me? Box 610."

The man frowned. "Are you on the list of names authorized for the box?"

"I must be. My dad wouldn't have asked me otherwise."

He nodded. "Let me check—box 610, did you say?"

"Yes, sir."

He used his index fingers to hunt and peck a few keys on a keyboard. "And what's your name?"

She hoped her father had used the same name he'd given to the Atlanta real estate agent—Bill Randolph. "Er...the name on the box is Randolph."

"Yes."

His confirmation sent her adrenaline spiking.

"But what's *your* name?"

"Uh...Carlotta." It was a longshot.

"Sorry ma'am, but that name isn't on the list."

"Maybe he has me in the system as Melanie?"

He squinted, then checked. "No female names listed on the account at all. Sorry."

"Maybe you could check to see if there's a letter from my father's doctor's office?" All she needed was a piece of mail that might lead her to a street address.

The guy pointed to one of the many hand-lettered signs posted on the counter. This one read "No mail given out over the counter. Don't ask."

"Oh. Okay, just to make sure I have the right box, can you confirm the street address on the account?"

"None listed," he said.

"Phone number?"

He frowned. "Come. Back. With. The. Key."

"I'll do that," she said congenially. She started to leave, then turned back. "One more question?"

The guy rolled his eyes.

She pulled out her phone and retrieved an image—a decade-old picture of Randolph and Valerie. "Just to make sure I'm in the right place, do you recognize my father? He's older now."

Her heart beat in her ears as the man peered at the photo. Then he shook his head. "No, that's not the man who picks up the mail for 610."

Her disappointment was acute. "Thanks. Maybe I do have the wrong place."

"But I recognize the woman."

Carlotta's head came up. "You do?"

"Yeah, she's been in with the man who picks up the mail. Pretty lady. Although, now that I think about it, I haven't seen her in a long time."

Carlotta thought her heart was going to hammer through her chest. "How often does this man come in?"

The guy gave her a quizzical look.

"Just wondering how piled up my dad's mail might be."

"I don't know—maybe once or twice a month?"

Crap. She didn't have that much time.

Another customer walked in carrying boxes, and the man went to help.

Her numb feet exited the store. Valerie was alive and somewhere nearby—or had been.

Carlotta stood there for a moment, paralyzed with elation and indecision. Now what? She needed to think. Moving blindly, she wheeled to go back to the coffee house.

And plowed hard into Jack Terry.

CHAPTER 8

"EXCUSE ME," Jack said, grasping her arm to keep her from falling. "I—"

His eyes bulged and any hope Carlotta had of him not recognizing her in the red wig evaporated.

"Carlotta? What the *hell* are you doing here?"

She shook herself free. "Good morning to you, too, Jack."

"Don't start batting your lashes, goddammit. *Talk.*"

"I don't know what you're implying," she said primly. "What are *you* doing here?" She narrowed her eyes. "Are you following me?"

His face went all mottled. "No. I'm not following you. I'm wondering why instead of having breakfast in bed in that outrageous suite of yours, you'd be loitering in a seedy part of town."

"I'm not loitering. I had coffee at a little place a couple of blocks away, bought a postcard, and came here to mail it." As proof, she pulled the postcard from her bag. "See?"

"Did you forget to mail it?"

He had a point. "N-No," she said, trying to recover. "I...decided to write something else on the postcard and mail it later."

He picked up a lock of the red wig. "And do you always get morning coffee in disguise?"

She pushed his hand away. "In the coffee shop, I saw those two guys who followed me and Peter, and I didn't want them to recognize me."

Jack squinted. "So you put on the disguise *after* you got to the coffee shop?"

Oh, crap. "Uh-hm."

He crossed his arms. "You're usually better at lying. But I'm going to give you a chance to come clean."

Her mouth watered to tell him the night she'd discovered the post office box receipt, he had been the first person she'd called because she'd wanted to share her jubilation. But he'd preempted her announcement with the news that Liz Fischer was carrying his baby. "Because you're so honest about everything, Jack?"

His shoulders fell. "Okay. We might as well have this conversation now."

She raised her eyebrows and waited.

"I'm sorry about the Liz situation." He sighed. "More than you know. It was a random night a couple of months ago—it didn't mean anything at the time. Maybe I was trying to prove something to myself, but that's no excuse. I was careless, and my actions hurt you. I'm sorry, Carlotta—truly."

Mixed emotions coursed through her as she processed the words of his apology. She'd practiced what she would say when they were alone, but all the clever, breezy retorts she had thought of abandoned her. "I'm so mad at you, Jack, for messing up everything."

Emotion flickered in his gold-colored eyes. "So am I." Then he straightened. "That said, you seem to have recovered pretty quickly. You didn't think to mention your engagement before I got on a plane to come out here? I have feelings, too, you know."

"No, I don't know," she corrected, her ire returning. The Great Impregnator had some nerve to be irritated at her for moving on. "Besides, when I called, I had a lifeless man on my hands."

"You'd better get used to that," he said with a dry smile.

She crossed her arms. "Peter might not be Mr. Exciting, but I don't have to worry about him getting another woman knocked up ten minutes after leaving my bed."

He pressed his lips together and had the good grace to dip his chin in concession. "Peter will give you the kind of life you deserve."

She knew Jack meant it as a compliment, but she was so confused about Peter's loyalties, it was lost on her. And the fact that she couldn't be one hundred percent happy about her engagement made her even more frustrated.

"So are you ready to tell me what you're doing here?" Jack said, nodding to the storefront.

"I already told you."

"Wrong. I know exactly why you're here, Carlotta."

She swallowed. "You do?"

"You found the piece of paper with the address on it in the dead man's mouth, then put it back, didn't you?"

Dead Johnson had a note in his mouth with this address on it? "You got me."

"I *knew* it. I told Coop no way you missed that."

Damn, she was slipping. But if Dead Johnson had that info, why was he following her? Why not do his own surveillance of the box? Wait—maybe he didn't have the box number.

"Jack, did you take a picture of the note?"

"You didn't?"

"I was in a hurry," she improvised.

Jack pulled out his phone, flipped through some images, then turned the screen toward her.

It was a small crumpled sticky note. She squinted at the writing, blurry from—presumably—saliva. Ick. It was the shipping store's address alright, but no box number.

Her breath rushed out in relief. Only she had it.

"So what did he say?"

She blinked. "Who?"

He gestured to the shipping store. "The guy working inside. I assume you showed him a picture of our dead man and asked if he knew him?"

"Er...actually, no. He had a line of customers, and my coffee was running through me, so I thought I'd come back later."

"Wow, so you're actually letting me do the police work?"

"What can I say, Jack? I have a tight...little...bladder." She batted her eyelashes.

Jack's eyes inadvertently swept over her, then he shook his finger. "You have to stop that. We're both...unavailable."

"The thing is, Jack, you always were." She gave him a little smile. "I'm going to find a bathroom."

"You don't want to go in with me?"

And have the guy ask her if she was back with the key to box 610? "No. But I'll get you some coffee if you'll pick me up and give me a ride back to the hotel."

"Deal. I take mine black."

"I remember," she said, then took off walking.

She replayed Jack's apology and how seamlessly they seemed to transition back to a teasing hands-off relationship. The uncertainty of where she stood with him before had been a constant pull on her heart. Maybe they were better at...*this*.

Her mind buzzed all the way back to the coffee house. The man at the shipping store had confirmed her mother was in the vicinity—or had been at one time. But who was the man who picked up the mail? Randolph in disguise? If so, the mail had been piling up for a while now while he sat in the Atlanta penitentiary.

At the coffee shop, she visited the bathroom and got a bolstering glimpse of her mother's signature, mulled the man's name she'd written on the wall, then ordered two coffees and danishes to go.

She waited only a few minutes before a neutral-colored SUV pulled to the curb and Jack waved.

"Nice rental," she said, climbing in. "Did the guy at the shipping store recognize Johnson?"

"Unfortunately, no. I'm thinking maybe he was supposed to

meet someone there."

"Or pick up a package?" Carlotta offered, trying not to feel guilty for attempting to throw Jack off track. "Maybe he mailed something to himself from Atlanta."

I asked the guy if there were any unclaimed packages, but he said if packages aren't picked up within two days, they get returned."

"Sounds like a dead end, no pun intended." She passed him a coffee and a danish.

"Thanks." Then he zeroed in on her arm and frowned. "That bracelet you're wearing is giving you a bad bruise."

She glanced at the growing discoloration on her wrist and sighed inwardly. "I'll be fine." Disconcerted, she took a sip of coffee, then changed the subject. "Where's Coop?"

"At the morgue. The M.E. invited him to observe the autopsy. He stuck around to learn the cause of death, or anything that could lead back to the guy's identity."

"What do you make of him having no fingerprints?"

"He's either a criminal, or someone who tracks criminals."

Either way, he could be connected to Randolph.

Jack took a drink from his coffee cup. "I remembered you said your real estate agent friend thought the ambiguity of the deed to the house where Johnson was staying pointed to a government agency."

"That's right. You blew me off."

"It didn't seem important at the time. But I left a message for Agent Wick in Atlanta to look into it, and told him we had an unidentified body."

"You think Johnson might be a GBI agent?"

"Maybe. Or working for the GBI. If so, it's possible the people he worked with don't know he's dead."

"Makes sense. Why do you think he had the note in his mouth of all places?"

"Maybe he put it between his teeth to free up his hands to try to get out of the safe? Hard to say."

Jack's phone rang and Carlotta glanced over to see Liz's name come up on the screen.

"Sorry, I need to get this," he said.

She nodded and leaned away from him, squashing the flash of resentment. She forced her mind away from the murmured conversation and back to the matter plucking at her.

How had Dead Johnson gotten the address for the shipping store? She hadn't shared it with anyone except Hannah, when they were searching online databases for a potential street address for Bill and Melanie Randolph.

Then a thought struck her—before coming to Las Vegas, she'd used her phone to find out as much as she could about the post office box address. Had the dead man hacked into her phone? Or Peter? Or someone at Mashburn & Tully?

Regardless, it was imperative she keep an eye on box 610. If only there was a way she could know when someone would *be* there to pick up mail. And she had less than a week.

Then she remembered something Jack had said—that packages had to be picked up within two days. Which meant customers were notified when packages arrived. In fact, she recalled seeing a sign to that effect.

"Okay, let me know if you have any updates," Jack was saying. "Okay, bye." When he disconnected the call, his expression was pinched.

"How's Liz?" she asked lightly.

"Liz is fine. But…I have some bad news."

She jerked her head around. "Randolph?"

Jack nodded. "He was jumped in the prison food hall and stabbed."

"Is he—?"

"He's alive in the prison infirmary under heavy guard; they'll move him if he recovers enough. But Liz said it doesn't look good."

"What happened? I thought he was in solitary confinement because a relative of one of his clients is housed there?"

"He was. The incident happened at meal time. The person you mentioned isn't implicated, but it's still under investigation."

She bit into her lip to stem rising tears. So after all this time, she and Wes still might never get to talk to Randolph, might never get answers. "If we fly back to Atlanta tonight, will they let us see him?"

"No. I'm sorry, they won't. And he's unconscious. But Liz said she'd call me with updates."

"She can't call me? Or Wes?"

"I guess she assumes you'd rather not hear from her. And she did try Wes, but she said he didn't pick up."

"Liz," Carlotta said with a strident little laugh. "No matter what happens, she's always in the mix, isn't she?"

Jack didn't seem to have a response. "I'll get you back to the hotel."

"Actually, can you drop me off at the post office up there on the left? I want to mail my postcard. I'll walk back to the hotel from there."

"I can wait while you get a stamp, Carlotta."

"Thanks, but I need to clear my head. And I can call Wes to let him know."

"Okay," he relented.

When he slowed the SUV, she hopped out. She could feel Jack watching her to make sure she went into the post office. When she got to the door, she turned and waved. The SUV pulled away. When it was out of sight, she turned and scanned the shops clustered around the post office. With Randolph ailing, all the more reason to seize any opportunity to find her mother.

A bookstore a few doors down caught her eye.

When she walked in, she was struck by how much bookstores had changed. In order to get to the actual books, she had to weave her way past kiosks of electronic devices, games, stuffed animals, and other tchotchkes. After some browsing, she found the section she was looking for.

Valerie had devoured glitz fiction—novels about the rich and famous leading decadent lives most people only dream of. She called them her brain candy. Carlotta often wondered if her mother used them as guidebooks for how to move in high society circles.

She recognized some of the authors' names from the books that used to adorn Valerie's nightstand. Randolph teased her about them, but often came home with a book he'd bought on his lunch hour he thought she would enjoy.

Despite the womanizing, he'd seemed to love Valerie. Had their love persevered being on the run the past ten years? And if so, did Valerie have any idea Randolph was now fighting for his life?

Pushing aside the melancholy thoughts, Carlotta selected several recent hardcover releases and paid for them, then lugged her load to the post office. From the wall of retail supplies, she selected a colorful cardboard box that would hold the books but also was larger than box 610 at the shipping store. She filled out the mailing label to M. Randolph while she waited in line. When she got to the counter, she hefted the box to the scale in front of the clerk.

"One postcard stamp, and I'd like to send this package overnight delivery, please."

The guy's eyebrows shot up. "It's gonna be expensive to send a package this heavy overnight."

"That's okay." She reasoned if she got a promotion and raise when she went back to Neiman's, she could pay down the towering balance on her credit card.

He scanned the address. "You know that's just a couple of miles from here."

She nodded.

"Lady, you could take it over in a limousine cheaper than this is gonna be."

"Still," she said, pleasantly.

He scratched his head. "Okay, but I can't send it without a return address."

She filled in the townhome's address—if the package wasn't picked up and found its way back to her in Atlanta, at least she'd have reading material for a while. When the clerk told her the delivery charge, she coughed, then swiped her beleaguered card. "What time will it be delivered?"

"Guaranteed by 10 a.m."

Carlotta thanked the man, then left, thinking of the supplies she would need for a stakeout. Binoculars, portable phone charger, snacks, water...

CHAPTER 9

"DUDE, IT'S BEEN twenty-one hours," Chance said, abandoning the joystick of the Mortal Kombat console. "Isn't that close enough, considering the different time zone and all?"

Wes looked up from the NBA Live game he was playing and squinted. "It doesn't work like that."

"Sniff it and see if it smells."

A cute girl walking by gave Chance a lethal look.

"He didn't mean you," Wes offered, but she was gone.

He shook his head at his snickering friend, then fished out his wallet and removed the fake driver's license. After glancing around to make sure no one was watching, he ran the plastic card under his nose and inhaled.

"Well? Does it stink?"

"I can't tell. Maybe."

"Let me take a whiff."

Wes handed it over. Chance held it under his big schnoz and inhaled deeply. "Mmm...smells like French fries."

"You mean like the fries you had for lunch?"

Chance sniffed again, then frowned. "Yeah, maybe I'm smelling my fingers."

"Wash your hands sometime, how about it?"

"I don't smell the card, though, so maybe it's okay to use it."

"And maybe I don't want to risk it," Wes said. "The guy

specifically said to wait twenty-four hours."

"Dude, I'm dying here. Let's go gamble."

"Nothing's stopping *you* from playing."

"It's not as much fun by myself," Chance whined. "And normally I'd kill time by going out and getting laid, but now there's Hannah, so…"

"Where is Hannah?"

"She said she went shopping with Carlotta."

"You don't believe her?"

"I don't know. I'm going to text her." He pulled out his phone.

Wes kept playing, with one eye on the clock, counting down the minutes until he could hit the poker tables. His backpack vibrated. Hoping it was Meg reaching out, he checked, but it was the phone Mouse had given him. Disappointed, he ignored it—it was nice Mouse wanted to stay in touch, but he'd ping the man back later. He'd ignored Liz's call, too—that whole fatherhood scare was still a little fresh.

"She's not responding," Chance said.

"Maybe she's busy."

"She hasn't responded all day."

Wes heard the injured note in his buddy's voice. He wouldn't be surprised if Hannah was out following Coop around the city, but he didn't want to dash Chance's dreams. "Don't get worked up about it."

"I love her, dude."

Wes abandoned his game. Chance looked like a little boy who'd lost his blankie. "That's cool, man, really. But you're not going to land Hannah if you act all needy and shit."

Chance worked his mouth from side to side. "But I *do* need her."

"But you can't *act* like you do, understand?"

"I guess so. But I'm miserable when she's not around. I think about her, like, all the time."

Wes could relate. Meg sat on his mind like a hat. "I get it, but you need to relax, man. Hannah digs your fat ass, don't mess it up by being a pain. She's on vacation, too."

"I know. I just can't shake this feeling that she's hiding something from me."

"I don't think she could get anything past you," Wes lied.

Chance nodded. "Yeah, you're right. I'm being hemorrhoid."

"I think you mean 'paranoid.'"

"Huh?"

"Never mind."

Wes's backpack vibrated again. He reached inside with the intention of turning off the phone Mouse gave him, then realized it was his main phone. He pulled it out and grinned. A text from Meg.

Hi. I'm guessing you put the bracelet on my teddy bear? Very pretty. Thank you.

His heart lifted. She liked it.

His phone vibrated with another text. *But this doesn't change anything.*

But it did change something—she was at least communicating with him. He hesitated, trying to think of something cool to text back and settled on *You're welcome. I'm in Vegas. Wish me luck.* And he added a few four-leaf clover emojis. Girls loved that shit.

A few seconds later his phone vibrated again. *You're not old enough to gamble.*

Wes frowned.

His phone lit up and his hope that Meg was calling was dashed when he saw Carlotta's name on the screen. Had she somehow found out about the money? Then he scoffed—now he was being a hemorrhoid. He connected the call. "Hey, Sis. What's up?"

"Hi, Wes." Her voice sounded tired. "Not good news, I'm afraid. Randolph was jumped and stabbed."

His grip tightened on the phone. "Is he okay?"

"He's alive in the prison infirmary, but it's serious."

"Should we go home?"

"They won't let us see him. But if the worst happens, we'll have to cut our trip short."

"So we can't see him until he's *dead*, is that what you're saying?"

"I suppose that's true. But it was his choice not to talk to us when he had the chance." She sighed. "Look, Wes, there's nothing we can do except hope he recovers. Try not to worry. Do something to keep your mind off everything. I'll let you know if I get any updates."

"Okay. Thanks, Sis." He disconnected the call, fighting tears of anger. Life just wasn't fair.

"You okay, dude?"

"Yeah." Wes swiped at his eyes. "C'mon, let's hit the tables."

"Fucking A, man. Hey, do you need some cash? I can spot you a few bills."

"Not necessary." Wes patted his jacket. "I got it covered."

CHAPTER 10

"THERE'S THE POSTAL TRUCK," Hannah said, bouncing in the driver's seat. Something on her jangled, but it could've been anything from her jewelry to the buckles on her studded black clothing.

Carlotta glanced away from the shipping store entrance and gave her friend a pointed look. "You might ease up on the caffeine—this could be a long day."

"I'm prepared," Hannah said, holding up an oddly shaped pink rubber object.

"What's that?"

"A portable urinal for women." She positioned it for demonstration. "So we can pee like a guy without leaving the car."

Carlotta scoffed. "When we need to pee, we'll take turns walking to the coffee house."

"Spoil sport. I brought it for you—I'm wearing a diaper."

Carlotta laughed, but she didn't doubt it. She knew Hannah was trying to cheer her up. There was still no word about Randolph's condition.

She lifted the binoculars to watch the packages being unloaded across the street. They were sitting in a rented SUV in a parking lot, with the nose of the vehicle facing the shipping store.

"Are you sure you'll recognize the box?" Hannah asked.

"Yeah. It had a colorful design, and I used a black marker to draw X's on all six sides. There it is." She released a pent-up breath, reminding herself this ruse was still a longshot. Randolph could've easily given a bogus contact number when he rented the box.

"This is so exciting," Hannah said, bouncing.

"This from someone who yesterday was lunching with a prince."

"A prince from some country no one's heard of. We could probably go there and be duchesses or some shit like that if we had enough money."

"You do have enough money," Carlotta said lightly.

"My parents have money," Hannah corrected. "I'm a slaving culinary student and underpaid body mover."

"How many boxes do you think the postal guy is taking inside?"

"Ten or so."

"I wonder how soon the man working there will call the customers to let them know they have a package."

"He doesn't seem to be overrun with customers."

"Hopefully Tuesdays are slow," Carlotta murmured.

When the postal truck left, she lowered the binoculars and relaxed in the seat. "Okay, the desk is manned until 6, so that's up to eight hours of waiting."

"Where does Peter think you are?"

"Out shopping with you. Where does Chance think you are?"

"Out shopping with you. He was suspicious last night, though."

"What time did you get back from your meeting?"

"About nine o'clock. Thanks again for letting me use your bathroom for a changeroo. Where were you and Peter?"

"At the Chihuly art gallery. He's trying to keep my mind off Randolph. And he's thinking about buying a chandelier for his house."

"Nice," Hannah said. "He must be pulling down some bank at Mashburn & Tully. Seven figures?"

"I've never asked," Carlotta said. "I assume he does well."

"You've never wondered how it is that the partners there are making so much money when your father's clients haven't been made whole?"

Carlotta squirmed. "Peter told me it's because the case was never prosecuted, that the firm was only responsible for repaying a small percentage of the claims, that Randolph is personally responsible for the bulk of the restitution." She sighed. "But that might never happen."

Hannah made a rueful noise. "Maybe when you find your mother, she'll be hoarding stacks of gold bars."

Carlotta was suddenly seized by the predicament she'd inadvertently put Hannah in by sharing information about her parents. "Hannah," she said carefully, "maybe you should sit this one out."

Hannah jerked her head around. "What do you mean?"

"I mean my mother is technically a fugitive. If you know where she is and you don't report it to authorities, you'll be aiding and abetting."

"So will you."

"But this is my family. It's a risk I'm willing to take."

"You're my family," Hannah said. "It's a risk I'm willing to take, too."

Carlotta's eyes watered as emotion thickened her throat.

"Oh, fuck, don't cry. I take it all back."

Carlotta laughed, then wiped at her lashes.

"Hey, I think he's making calls," Hannah said, lifting her binoculars.

Carlotta lifted hers and focused. Sure enough, the man at the counter was making phone calls, then setting aside the packages one at a time.

"There's your package," Hannah said.

Carlotta held her breath.

He tapped on the keyboard and after consulting the computer

screen, punched in a number.

"He's calling," Hannah said.

He seemed to be waiting…and listening. Probably to a ringing phone. "No one's answering," Carlotta murmured with a sinking feeling.

"There—his lips are moving. He's talking to someone!"

But he wasn't taking breaks like someone listening to another person on the other end would. Then he hung up.

"He left a message." Carlotta lowered her binoculars and sighed. "Dammit. That voice message could be sitting on a burner cell phone hidden somewhere in the Buckhead house."

"Try to be positive. Think of all the little things that worked out in order for you to be sitting here."

"Ten years after the fact," Carlotta said. "And if Randolph had just given me the address when I talked to him in the pen, I wouldn't be jumping through these hoops. And look at the hoops you and I both jumped through just to get in and talk to him in the first place." She grunted in frustration. "He could've made this a thousand times easier."

"Maybe there's a reason he's reluctant for you to reunite with your mother. You said she was an alcoholic."

Carlotta nodded. "I've wondered if she still drinks, or if she's gotten worse."

"It had to be stressful for her to be away from you and Wesley."

"I'd like to think so," Carlotta said, "but Valerie wasn't what you'd call 'maternal.' She wasn't a bad mother, just…inattentive." She turned in her seat. "What's your mother like?"

"Ha—I *wish* my mother was an alcoholic. She's so uptight."

"Your sisters I met at the wedding trade show seemed nice."

"Uh-huh."

"You're not going to tell me anything about your family?"

"Uh-uh."

Carlotta crossed her arms. "We need to talk about something

for eight hours."

"Have you popped Peter's cherry yet?"

"Hannah," she scolded, but she couldn't help laughing.

"I take that as a 'no.'"

"We're working our way up to it," Carlotta murmured. "We've both been preoccupied."

"Any word on the dead guy's identity?"

"Not yet. Jack and Coop are working on it." She studied her cuticles. "Speaking of Jack…"

"I'm listening."

"He and I talked. About the baby."

"And?"

"And he said he was sorry he hurt me, that it was one night with Liz and it wasn't supposed to be any more than that. He said something cryptic, that maybe he'd been trying to prove something to himself."

"Oh, no, he didn't pull the non-apology-apology trick, did he?"

"The what?"

"In one breath, he said he was sorry, but in the next he tried to make you think he slept with Liz because he was trying to prove he's not in love with you. So really it's *your* fault Liz is pregnant."

Carlotta frowned. "Damn him. I can't believe I fell for that. I actually felt sorry for him." She banged her fist on the dashboard. "What an asshole. He even insinuated that Peter is a cold fish."

"Well, I have to agree with Detective Asshole on that one. Wait—we have a customer."

Carlotta yanked her binoculars back to her face to see a person opening the door of the shipping business. "It's a woman. But we're not sure who we're looking for, so keep an eye on what she carries out."

"You keep watching," Hannah said. "Someone just parked and is walking past the car, so I'm pretending I'm on my phone."

Carlotta tensed. "Do they look suspicious? Just because we

didn't see anyone following us doesn't mean they didn't."

"No. He looks like a tourist, probably trolling for drugs—or a hooker. We're good, he didn't even look this way."

"*Phew*—good."

"We were careful. The car's in my name. And do you really think someone would make you leaving the hotel in that blond wig?"

"I guess it depends on the sophistication of the people who might be watching me."

It occurred to her if Peter was reporting back to someone on her actions, he could report she was good at evading detection with costumes.

A movement at the door caught her attention. "The customer's leaving." She trained the binoculars on the woman's hands, then sighed. "But she's carrying only a few envelopes." She lowered the binoculars.

"At least we know our system works," Hannah said. "No way is someone getting out of there with your package without us seeing them. Here comes another customer. This one's carrying a box."

And so it went for several hours—customers coming and leaving, each without the package. The girls ate snacks and made coffee runs and took bathroom breaks. They talked about everything from Hannah's new loft apartment in Atlanta to shows they were watching to when and if Carlotta should tell Wes about what she was doing.

"If I find our mother, then of course I'll tell him," she said.

"And if you don't find your mother?"

"Then he doesn't have to be subjected to yet another disappointment."

"Wes might be stronger than you give him credit for."

"I see glimpses of maturity," Carlotta admitted. "But when it comes to our parents, I think he's still a nine-year-old boy desperate for Mommy and Daddy to come home. I mean, that sad little Christmas tree in the living room says it all, doesn't it?"

"That's a little messed up," Hannah agreed.

This exercise had resurrected a lot of memories of what life had been like after her parents had left—the initial panic, then slipping into survival mode, then the slow, sickening realization she and Wes were on their own. Looking back, she didn't know how they'd made it through. But they had—and they deserved answers.

She'd never forgive Randolph if he died and took those answers to the grave.

"At least Wes is trying to have some fun," Carlotta said. "He said he and Chance were going to an amusement park today."

"At least they're syncing their stories," Hannah said dryly.

Carlotta ignored the niggle of worry in her stomach where Wes was concerned. Instead she imagined the look on his face when she told him she'd found their mother.

When the clock crept into the last hour, though, her energy was fading—along with her optimism. She had resigned herself to coming back the next day for more of the same, when a wave of customers arrived who must have left work at five. Both she and Hannah were scanning frantically to keep up with the activity.

Suddenly, a brown package delivery truck pulled up in front of the door, blocking their view.

"Shit. What do we do now?" Hannah asked.

"You keep your eye on the customers who exit to the left, and I'll watch the customers who exit to the right."

While the driver unloaded packages from the rear of his truck onto a hand cart, the girls were glued to the activity of the customers emerging from behind either side of the truck.

"Wait," Hannah said. "Guy in the blue shirt—I think he's carrying your package."

Carlotta yanked her binoculars to the left, scanning for the person Hannah described. Man...wearing a blue shirt...and he was definitely carrying her package.

"That's it." Carlotta's heart raced.

"Holy shit, he's coming this way."

They lowered their binoculars and watched the man walk within a car's length of the SUV. He was perhaps forty, fit and well-groomed, with neat brown hair. He wore dark sunglasses and moved with quiet authority. He stopped next to a white BMW sedan parked in the row behind them, and perused the package, even gave it a shake.

"Do you recognize him?" Hannah whispered, as if he could hear them.

"No."

"Are you going to confront him?"

"No," Carlotta said. "It would be too easy for him to say he doesn't know Randolph or Valerie and simply leave. Let's follow him."

"I thought you'd never ask," Hannah said, yanking her seatbelt down for a click.

Carlotta did the same. "Wait until he gets in his car before you turn over the engine so we don't attract attention."

"Got it. This is so exciting!" Hannah whacked the steering wheel, blasting the horn.

The man's head whipped around to stare at their car.

"Sorry," Hannah whispered.

"Just stay calm. No sudden movements."

After a few seconds, he unlocked his car and set the package in the back seat, then climbed behind the wheel. When the car backed out of the parking spot, Carlotta said, "Now."

Hannah turned over the engine and put both hands on the wheel like a driver's ed student. "Go?"

"Yes, go! He's turning right. Try to put a car or two between us if you can."

They pulled out of the parking lot and followed the BMW at a respectable distance...to the grocery store where they waited for forty-five minutes for him to emerge. Then to the pharmacy,

80

where they waited another thirty minutes.

"He's getting in all his errands," Hannah grumbled.

Next he drove to a casual sit-down restaurant chain.

"Shoot," Carlotta said. "How long will this take?"

"No, look—he's pulling into the takeout parking."

Sure enough, he emerged a few minutes later carrying two large bags.

"You don't think he's noticed us, do you?" Hannah asked.

"No. You're doing great, like you've been stalking people all of your life."

"Thanks," Hannah said happily.

When he left the restaurant, they followed him to a residential area of older neighborhoods and mid-size cookie-cutter houses. Since traffic was lighter, it was harder to keep him in sight without being too obvious. After a series of turns, the car veered down a street that frankly, looked like all the others around it.

"Welcome to Stepfordville," Hannah muttered.

Dusk was starting to set when the BMW slowed and turned onto a concrete driveway in front of a small ranch house. The garage door opened, the car disappeared inside, then the door lowered.

"Drive by the house," Carlotta directed. But she could barely get the words out, her throat was so tight.

The home looked well-kept but was otherwise unremarkable. There were two lights on in the house, and as they drove by, another one came on.

"Turn around and go back."

Hannah maneuvered the SUV around a cul-de-sac, then headed back. When they reached the house again, Carlotta said, "Pull into the driveway."

"Okay." Hannah sounded wary, but complied, then brought the car to a stop. "Now what?"

"Now," said Carlotta, opening the door, "I'm going to knock."

"Are you sure about this?"

"No," she said, then quietly closed the car door.

From the driveway, a narrow rock path led to the front door of the house. She could barely hear her footsteps against the stones because the blood was roaring in her ears. Carlotta stepped up to the door, lifted her hand, and rang the doorbell.

And waited.

CHAPTER 11

WES NURSED A RUSH OF ADRENALINE when the dealer slid the white button to the front of the sizable pile of chips he'd accumulated. The dealer button meant he'd act last on the deal, which is the position he liked best, especially at a four-hand table.

Not that he needed the advantage—he'd pretty much been playing perfect poker in the room all day. He'd started slow the night before, buying only a few hundred dollars' worth of chips, but as his luck and confidence had grown, he'd pulled more cash from his jacket to hand to the dealer in exchange for chips of larger denominations.

He knew it was unlucky to count his chips before taking them to the cashier, but he guessed he'd already doubled his money.

And it was only Tuesday.

He wondered if other players in the room were talking about him yet—the new guy who couldn't seem to lose. He couldn't wait to tell Meg that not only did he play in one of the biggest poker rooms in Vegas, but he won big. His backpack vibrated and he checked to see if she or Carlotta were trying to reach him, but it was only Mouse's phone again. Irritated, Wes powered it down.

"Whatcha drinkin'?" a busty waitress asked.

"Uh, Coke Zero."

"C'mon, it's on the house," she said with a wink. "Live a little."

"Okay. I'll have a beer." He pulled out his wallet to flash his fake driver's license. "I'm twenty-six."

"So I see. But we don't card in here—we know you were carded at the door." She grinned and said she'd be right back.

"I think she likes you," Chance said from the next seat. "She didn't offer me a free drink."

"You can have mine when she brings it."

"You've taken enough of my money," Chance groused. "The least you can do is get me a beer. You're on fire, man."

"Why don't you find a black jack table?" He didn't like taking his friend's money—plus Chance was lousy at poker.

"I might, after this hand. Dude, that five-hundred-dollar investment was worth it, huh?"

"Yeah. I guess it passed the sniff test."

"Place your blinds," the dealer announced.

The two players to the right of Chance would act on the hand first, so they placed the small blind and big blind bets, five hundred and one thousand, respectively.

"Dealing," the dealer announced.

Two cards were dealt face-down to all four players. Wes curled up the corners of his cards—jack of spades and ten of hearts—and was satisfied. The first position player called to the big blind, the second player checked, and Chance folded—much to Wes's relief. Wes called the big blind, and raised five hundred. Players one and two called his raise.

"Burn," the dealer announced, and put the top card from the deck under Chance's folded cards. "Here comes the flop."

He dealt three cards face-down on the table, then flipped them over and spread them out: five of hearts, jack of hearts, and queen of diamonds. They were community cards each player could use to build a winning hand.

Wes liked his pair of jacks. Player one bet another five hundred, player two called, Wes called and raised another five. Player one folded. Player two called his raise.

The dealer burned another card. "Here's the turn."

He dealt a fourth community card face-up—the jack of

diamonds. Wes schooled his face so he didn't betray his three of a kind.

The other remaining player hesitated. His pile of chips was getting smaller and Wes knew he was trying to decide whether to walk away with rent money or maybe lose it all. Finally he bet one hundred. Wes called and raised five hundred. The guy squirmed, then called.

The dealer burned another card. "There's the river."

He dealt a fifth community card—queen of clubs.

Bummer. With two queens showing, his opponent could have three or even four of a kind, both of which would beat his three jacks. But those were the only two hands that could beat him. The guy's leg was jumping—his tell. He didn't have it.

The guy bet his last seven hundred. Wes called.

"What do you have, sir?" the dealer asked Wes's opponent. Since he placed the last bet, it was his game to lose.

"Three of a kind."

Wes's heart dropped, until the guy turned over two fives to go with the five in the flop.

The dealer gave Wes a questioning look.

"Three jacks," Wes said, turning over his pocket cards.

The other guy's shoulders dropped and Chance whooped. "Man, you can't lose!"

Wes allowed himself a grin as the dealer pushed the pot to him—he had to admit it felt pretty good to be catching good cards at a high-limit table in a swanky poker room. He reached inside his jacket, pulled out a Franklin, and handed it to the dealer with a wink. The guy thanked him for the tip and folded it into his pocket.

The busty waitress was back. "Here's that beer, honey." She set it in front of him and gave him a panoramic view of her cleavage.

"And here's something for you," Wes said, pulling out another hundred for her.

"Thank you!" She beamed and tucked the bill in her little apron, then reached for his hand and turned it over. "This is my number—call me later if you want to hang out."

Wes stared at the phone number she'd written on his palm in black ink. "Okay."

She gave him a little wave before moving off.

He watched her wiggle away and grunted. Meg who?

"We oughtta move out here," Chance said. "There's so much freaking money floating around. And with your card skills, man, you'd be rich in no time."

Wes pursed his mouth and thought about Mouse accusing him of skipping town. The man was right—he didn't have much keeping him in Atlanta. His dad might not make it and didn't want anything to do with him anyway...Carlotta was engaged to Peter...and Meg wasn't giving him any hope.

"Let's do it," Wes said with a shrug. "In fact, why bother going home at all? I love this place!"

"Excuse me, sir."

Wes turned around to see two security guards in a wide-legged stance. This couldn't be good.

"We need you to come with us."

"What—"

Before he could get another word out, they had each grabbed an arm and were helping him along.

"Get my chips," he yelled back to Chance.

"That won't be happening," one of the guards said. "Pick up your feet."

Since the alternative was to be dragged, Wes began to trot to keep up with the behemoths. His face burned as he was paraded through the casino while everyone stared and pointed.

He was escorted down a long hallway to a grim chamber that was as intimidating as any police interrogation room. The security guards ordered him to sit in a chair behind a table and keep his hands in sight. They put his backpack in a wire cage as if it was an animal that might try to escape.

"Slow crime day, guys?" he asked.

"Shut up," they said in unison.

A few minutes later the door opened and a craggy-faced man wearing a gray sport coat walked in with a scowl and a swagger. "What's your name, son?"

Wes swallowed hard. "Wesley. Wren."

"Where are you from?"

"Atlanta."

"Atlanta, Georgia. Mighty hot there."

Wes pursed his mouth and nodded, then realized with a thud he should've told them the town on his fake ID—Ozark, Alabama. Crap.

"I'm Captain Pace of the Las Vegas Police Department."

"Captain?" Wes gave a little laugh. "No offense, but don't you think all of this is a little overkill?"

"Overkill?"

"I mean, there are no victims here. I spent a lot of money in this casino, and I won a lot of money. And I tipped really well—ask anybody. The way I see it, this is a win-win situation."

"Is that right?" the captain asked, seeming amused.

Wes was glad the guy was lightening up. "In fact, I'll forego my winnings if you'll let me walk out of here with the money I brought with me."

"That sounds like a deal," the man said with a nod.

Wes exhaled in relief. "Just don't tell my sister."

"Is your sister involved in this?"

"No—not at all. And this has nothing to do with the dead guy that showed up in her hotel room."

The man frowned. "Dead guy?"

A hot flush began to creep up Wes's face. "Like I said—no connection."

"Okay, stand up."

Wes pushed to his feet. "I appreciate you being so

understanding."

"Turn around, please."

Before Wes knew what was happening, the captain had pulled his hands behind his back and snapped on cuffs.

"Guys, I was just having a little fun. And you gotta admit—it looks real."

"Wesley Wren, you're under arrest for possession of counterfeit money and fraud."

Wes's head came around. "What? Did you say counterfeit *money?*"

"You have the right to remain silent and refuse to answer questions," the man continued. "Anything you say may be used against you…"

CHAPTER 12

AS CARLOTTA STOOD in front of the door, waiting to see if anyone would answer, a tangle of scenarios wound through her head. What if her mother opened the door? What would she say to Valerie? And would her mother hug her, or turn her away?

What if the man answered? She needed to be ready to explain her presence. And how was he connected to her parents?

What would she do if no one answered? Camp out on the driveway until someone emerged? She couldn't very well break down the door...although Hannah probably could.

Under the blond wig, her scalp crawled. A layer of perspiration covered her body and her heart was beating so fast, she felt faint. She had just decided she should probably sit down when the door knob rattled.

Carlotta sucked in a sharp breath.

The door opened...to reveal a young girl with long, dark hair wearing a flowered sundress. "Hello," she said, looking up at Carlotta with a wary expression.

Carlotta's momentary confusion gave way to a logical explanation—the man was probably an employee of Randolph's, hired to do errands, and this was the man's home and family.

"Hi," Carlotta said. But her next words were cut off by the appearance of the man they'd been following.

"Come away from the door," the man said to the girl. Then he looked at Carlotta with a guarded look. "Who are you and why have you been following me?" The girl hovered behind him.

Carlotta chose her words carefully. "Randolph sent me to find you. But I only had the P.O. box number."

"So you sent the package?"

She nodded. "I need to talk to you." She hoped the words didn't sound as desperate as she felt.

"I think you should go," the man said, starting to close the door.

"Carlotta?" called a woman's voice inside. "I need you."

As soon as she heard it, Carlotta recognized her mother's voice. The sound was a shock to her system. She opened her mouth, but no words came out of her constricted throat.

"I'm coming, Mommy," the little girl said, then disappeared.

Even as her mind reeled, Carlotta realized the door was closing and along with it, the chance to find the answers to questions that haunted her every step for the past decade. She put her hand in the opening and grunted in pain when the door mashed her fingers. When the door opened a few inches and the man's face reappeared, she maintained her hold on the door frame, despite the throbbing.

"I'm not leaving," she said evenly.

They remained locked in combative eye contact for a few seconds, then the man conceded with a nod and opened the door.

She stepped inside a cramped foyer, gulping air to supply her trembling body. As Carlotta fought to stay upright, she vaguely registered muted lighting and neutral wall colors. Waist-high wood paneling throughout dated the house, but added a quality feel. The floors were wood, too, although she caught a glimpse of terra cotta tile in what she presumed was the kitchen.

"This way," the man said.

She followed him toward the sound of a television into a small but comfortable room where a woman sat in a club chair, going through the box of books Carlotta had sent and talking low with the little girl. At their approach, the woman swung her head toward them, and Carlotta stumbled. It could have been her and her mother when she was that age.

Valerie Randolph was still beautiful, but her once-dark chic hair was overgrown and generously streaked with silver. Her cheekbones were still high and sharp, and her skin was smooth. Her trim form, clad in slacks and one of her signature turtlenecks, was the figure of a much younger woman.

The smile she gave them framed her brown eyes with fine lines. "We have a visitor?"

With a start, Carlotta remembered she was wearing a blond wig—of course her mother wouldn't recognize her at first glance.

"Yes, Melanie," the man said. "Mr. Randolph sent her to check on you."

The expression of confusion and panic on her mother's face set off warning bells in Carlotta's mind.

"Where is Randolph?" her mother asked, looking all around the room, as if he might be hiding behind a lamp.

"He's away for a while, remember?" the man said gently.

"My daddy is gone a lot," the little girl said matter-of-factly to Carlotta.

When she spoke, a gap between her front teeth was noticeable—and familiar. Carlotta saw it every time she looked in the mirror.

She swallowed hard as the realization hit her. She and Wesley had a little sister. She looked to be about nine—the same age as Wes when their parents had disappeared. Which meant her mother had been pregnant when they left, or had become pregnant soon after.

"I like your dress," Carlotta said to the little girl.

The girl eyed her suspiciously.

"Say thank you, Carlotta," the woman admonished.

"Thank you," the little girl said, then she leaned closer. "My real name is Priscilla, but Mom calls me Carlotta sometimes. I think it's someone she used to know."

Carlotta nodded, unable to speak.

"I want Randolph to come back," her mother said in a

childlike voice.

The little girl walked back to the chair. "He will, Mom. As soon as he can."

Her mother nodded and held up one of the books Carlotta had sent. "Randolph bought this for me today. He always buys me books." She smiled, opened the book and sat back in the chair, already preoccupied.

Carlotta turned to the man. "What's wrong with her?"

"Mr. Randolph didn't tell you?"

She shook her head, filled with dread.

He sighed. "Melanie has dementia. The doctors think it's early onset Alzheimer's, but they're not sure."

Carlotta bit down hard on her tongue to quell the sob that formed in her throat. *No.*

"I'm sorry," he said. "I can tell from your reaction that you must know Melanie."

Carlotta nodded, blinking back tears. "Yes. We used to be...close."

The man adopted a defensive stance. "I just realized I didn't catch your name." His voice was once again full of distrust, his body language, rigid.

Across the room, her mother's laugh rang out in merriment. "Why, that's Carlotta, of course. Why on earth are you wearing a wig, sweetheart?"

Everyone froze.

Knowing her mother recognized her sent elation coursing through Carlotta's chest. She went to Valerie and knelt next to the chair. "Hi, Mom," she said gently. "It's so good to see you. How are you?"

"I'm fine, dear, can't you see?" She touched Carlotta's cheek and looked concerned. "Why are you crying? Peter isn't being mean to you, is he?"

Carlotta smiled through her tears. "No. Peter is good to me."

"Where is your engagement ring?" her mother asked, touching

Carlotta's hand.

"It's in a safe place," she assured her.

"Good. I worry about a girl in high school wearing such a valuable piece of jewelry."

Sadly, Carlotta realized her mother's mind had rewound to the time before she and Randolph had left.

Valerie smiled. "Is the wig for drama class?"

"That's right," Carlotta said, touching her blond hair.

"You were always such an entertainer. And a beautiful dancer. Your ballet teacher says you could be on Broadway." Valerie sighed. "Of course, not if you marry Peter."

"You don't want me to marry Peter?"

"I don't want you to give up your dreams...like I did."

Carlotta was rapt. Her mother had never talked about a life she might've had if she hadn't married Randolph.

"I take ballet," Priscilla announced to Carlotta, then wedged herself between the two women, crowding out Carlotta. "Aren't I a good dancer, Mommy?"

Valerie smiled lovingly at Priscilla. "Yes, you're a wonderful dancer, didn't you just hear what I said?" She stroked the little girl's hair. "Your ballet teacher says you could be on Broadway someday." Then Valerie looked confused, as if two memories had collided.

"Mom," Carlotta said, hoping to bring her back to the present. "Wesley is with me."

Her mother squinted. "Is that a friend of yours, dear?"

She choked back a sob. Wesley would be devastated if their mother didn't recognize him. "No, Mom, Wesley is my little brother. Remember?"

Valerie picked up a brush from a table next to the chair and began to comb the little girl's hair. "Your daddy and I have talked about having another child, and if it's a boy, we'll name him Wesley. Would you like to have a brother or a sister?"

Priscilla made a thoughtful noise. "Not really. I like things the way they are."

The girl was precocious, Carlotta observed.

"But I get lonely sometimes," Valerie said. "Your father is gone so much."

"But he brings you nice books." The little girl talked as if she were used to cheering up her mother.

"Yes, he does." Valerie said, stroking the brush through the little girl's hair, over and over, like she used to do when Carlotta was little.

"Mom," Carlotta said, speaking quietly, "before Dad left, did he give you anything to keep safe for him?"

Valerie acted as if she hadn't heard her, just kept brushing Priscilla's hair.

"Mom, this is really important," Carlotta said. "Did Randolph hide anything, maybe papers from Mashburn & Tully, the place he used to work? Try to remember."

Valerie didn't react, seemed to be in her own world.

Priscilla turned haughty eyes to Carlotta. "She's not going to answer. She doesn't know you."

Feeling like an intruder, Carlotta pushed to her feet to walk back to the man who had been watching everything with a somewhat befuddled expression.

"You're Melanie's daughter?"

"Yes. My name is Carlotta."

"That explains a lot. Priscilla is accustomed to answering to either name."

"She looks very much like I did at that age."

"And Mr. Randolph is your father?"

"Yes. We've been out of touch for a long time, until recently."

"I'm Birch, by the way," he said, extending his hand. "I live here and take care of things for the Randolphs."

She shook his hand. "Thank you, Birch, for looking after my mother. How long have you known them?"

"Going on two years now. Mr. Randolph is in trouble, isn't he?"

"He was arrested in Atlanta…and while he was in custody, he was attacked. He's…not well."

Birch covered his mouth with his hand. "Atlanta—is that where you live?"

"Yes."

He sighed. "It has something to do with his day trading, doesn't it?"

So that's what her father had been up to. "It's connected to his former job," she hedged. "In the short time Randolph and I talked, he said he had proof that would exonerate him of the charges, but he didn't tell me what it was. Do you know if he gave my mother something for safekeeping?"

Birch shook his head. "No. I've always had a feeling something wasn't on the up and up with their situation, but I didn't want to pry. Bill pays me well, and Melanie and Prissy are like family to me."

Suddenly Priscilla appeared at his side. "Mom is asleep."

Carlotta looked over to see her mother had dozed off in the chair with a tiny smile on her face. She drank her in—it was surreal to be near her. And heartbreaking to know she wasn't well.

"I'll get her a blanket," Birch said, then left the room.

Priscilla looked up. "So, you're my sister?"

She smiled down. "So it seems. My name is Carlotta."

"Mom gets us mixed up."

Carlotta nodded, then pointed to a mirror on the wall and leaned down so their faces were side by side. "See?" She grinned to reveal the gap in her front teeth.

Priscilla showed her gap. "We have the same smile."

"That's right. And when I take off my wig, we'll look like twins."

"We can't be twins," the girl said pointedly. "You're old."

Carlotta blinked. "I'm not that old."

The girl's eyes narrowed. "You made Mommy upset."

"I didn't mean to."

"But you did anyway. You really should go now." Priscilla stared at her, unblinking.

Carlotta bit down on her tongue. Little Miss Priss was a force to be reckoned with.

Birch returned with the blanket and tucked it around their mother's sleeping form. "Are you hungry, Prissy?"

She nodded.

Birch looked at Carlotta. "Would you like to have dinner with us?"

"She has to go," Priscilla said, swinging her gaze back to Carlotta. "Don't you?"

She was going to have to tread carefully around this one. "Actually, a friend is waiting in the car. Would it be alright if I come back tomorrow?"

"We'll be busy," Priscilla said, crossing her arms.

"Prissy, mind your manners," the man chided.

"It's fine," Carlotta assured him, then nodded toward the door. "Goodbye, Prissy. I hope you and I will become good friends."

"Birch is the only person who calls me Prissy."

"Good to know," Carlotta said with a nod. "I'll see you again soon."

"Or not." Priscilla turned and marched out of the room.

The girl knew how to make an exit.

"I'm sorry about that," Birch said. "She's actually a sweet child. Very smart—maybe too smart."

"She's protective of her mother, and that's understandable. She seems mature for her age."

"Unfortunately, she has to be," Birch murmured.

A pang of sympathy barbed through her chest. Randolph and Valerie's actions had forced all their children to grow up sooner than they were prepared for.

Carlotta gave her sleeping mother one last look and touched

her silky hair, just to prove to herself this wasn't a dream, like the trip she'd once taken across time thanks to some powerful painkillers. In that epic dream, she'd gotten a glimpse of what her life might've been like if her parents hadn't left her and Wesley. In that version of her life, her mother had been a high-functioning alcoholic...but wasn't that preferable to the future Valerie was facing now?

She walked to the door with Birch. "There's so much I need to discuss with you. Can we exchange phone numbers?"

"Of course."

"Also," Carlotta said, choosing her words carefully, "I don't mean to frighten you, but my father has enemies who might be looking for something to leverage against him. I need to figure out how to safely relocate my mother and sister. In the meantime, be careful who you open the door to."

"Says the woman who practically forced her way inside," Birch said.

"I'm sorry. But I hope you understand why I had to."

"I'm not sure I understand everything that's going on, but I know I can trust you. Mr. Randolph said this day might come— that the Carlotta Melanie talked about would show up. He was right."

If Randolph had intermittently monitored the listening device he'd planted in the kitchen of the townhome, he must've known she was determined to get to the bottom of their disappearance.

"I'll be back tomorrow," she promised. "Call me if anything out of the ordinary happens."

"You mean anything *else* out of the ordinary."

Instinctively, she liked Birch. If Randolph had chosen him to live here and watch Valerie and Priscilla in his absences, he must've had a great deal of confidence in the man.

She said goodbye, and when she walked outside, dusk was fading to darkness. The cool night air bathed her face as she made her way back to the SUV on wobbly legs. Hannah was on the phone, but put it down and sprang across the console to pull the door handle.

Carlotta climbed inside, feeling spent. This had to go down as the most momentous day of her life.

"I was getting ready to call the cavalry," Hannah said. "What the fuck happened?"

Carlotta leaned her head back and gave Hannah the five-minute version.

"You have a *sister*? Holy crap, your life is a telenovela."

"I know." She pulled on her seatbelt. "Let's get back to the hotel."

Hannah stared. "You found your mother and you're leaving?"

"I have to get Wes and bring him back here. I can't deal with this alone and he deserves to know."

Her phone rang, and Wes's name flashed on the screen. "Wait—this is Wes. Oh, Hannah, he's going to be so happy." She connected the call. "Hi, Wes. I was just going to call you. I have such good news."

"Sorry to cut you short, Sis, but I don't have much time...and my news isn't that great."

She gripped the phone. "What's wrong?"

"I've been arrested."

Her stomach fell. "Arrested? For what?"

"Oh, shit," Hannah muttered.

"It's complicated," Wes said. "Can you call Jack? And Liz?"

Carlotta closed her eyes. "Okay."

"Thanks, Sis. Now you can tell me your good news."

Carlotta massaged the headache exploding behind her eyes. "I'll tell you later. Hold tight." She disconnected the call and let the numbness overtake her.

Minus one hundred.

CHAPTER 13

WES DUCKED TO AVOID a turd being flung through the air. He thought the holding cells in Atlanta were scary, but they were nothing compared to the holding cells in Clark County, Nevada. His cellmates ran the gamut from drunks to punks, from streakers to tweakers. At any given time, someone was singing or screaming or banging their head on the wall. One guy sat in the corner holding imaginary knitting needles, allegedly making a sweater for Hugh Grant.

The poop tossing, although gross and disturbing, was appropriate for the occasion, however, because no matter how Wes sliced and diced his situation, he was in deep shit.

Underage in a casino? *Check.*

Using a fake driver's license? *Check.*

Placing bets with counterfeit money? *Check, check.*

But even more scary than the charges pending, was the knowledge that he'd paid off his loan shark with counterfeit money. No wonder Mouse had been calling.

"Wes!"

He turned his head to see Chance standing on the other side of the bars, craning. Wes bolted up and went over. "Hey, man."

Chance's eyes bulged. "You're counterfeiting money?"

"No." He glanced around. "Keep your voice down. Wait—how'd you know about the money?"

"Because my buddy Nick just called me screaming that you stiffed him with five fake Franklins, and now his bank is all over his ass."

After registering mild surprise a criminal like Nick would use a bank, he winced—The Carver wasn't the only bad dude he'd paid with the phony baloney.

"What were you thinking, man? Even a dumbshit like me knows counterfeiting is federal. That's serious fucking time."

"As opposed to dealing drugs?" Wes said dryly.

"Man, the U.S. government doesn't give a rat's ass about a two-bit pill pusher. But they ain't playing when it comes to their dough."

"I didn't know it was fake."

"Where the freak did you get it?"

"I can't tell you. Can you smooth things over with Nick?"

"I covered the five hundred."

"Thanks, man."

"But you got worse problems. Dillon Carver is out to get you."

Wes's knees felt rubbery, so he held on to the bars. "Before I left town, I paid off my debt to The Carver with some of that money."

"So I heard. Dillon said you got him in a world of trouble with his dad."

"So I have a beating coming if I ever get out of here?"

"A beating? Wes, Dillon put a hit out on your scrawny ass."

Wes swayed. "A hit?"

"Yeah, man. This is for real." Chance looked past Wes. "Is that guy pretending to knit?"

Wes snapped his fingers to bring Chance back to the crisis at hand. "I thought I saw Leonard outside the hotel."

Chance's eyes popped. "Are you sure it was him?"

"No. But do you think Dillon sent him to smoke me?"

"If it's Leonard, he didn't come to Vegas to see Britney Spears."

Wes jammed his hand into his hair. "What should I do, man?"

"Stay in as long as you can. The freaks in here are better than what's waiting for you out there."

Wes nodded. "Meanwhile, if anyone asks, I got the fake bills in a poker game back home, okay?"

"Yeah, okay."

"Visiting time is over, ladies," a guard said, walking up to the door. "Wren, your lawyer is on the phone." The guy leered. "She sounds hot."

"She is," Chance said, "and Wes balls her all the time."

"Hey," Wes said, punching Chance's arm. "I don't anymore. And this isn't the time to talk about hot ass."

"It's always time to talk about hot ass," Chance said.

"I'll be sure to tell Hannah you said that," Wes said as the guard unlocked the door.

"Don't do that," his buddy said, back-pedaling. "She and Carlotta are on their way down."

"Stand back," the guard shouted to the masses. He clanged a baton against the metal to clear enough space for Wes to get out.

"I'm not talking to Carlotta. And keep your trap shut."

"I'm as silent as the grave."

Wes sighed. "Did you have to mention the word 'grave'?"

"Sorry. Hang in there."

When they got to the end of the hallway, the guard sent Chance in one direction and led Wes in another. Wes's feet felt like buckets of cement as he walked into a room lined with phone banks.

"Number three," the guard said. "You got ten minutes."

Wes picked up the grubby handset. "Liz?"

"Yes, it's me, Wes. Carlotta called, said you'd been arrested in Vegas. She said you wouldn't tell her why. Did you get caught soliciting?"

"Uh, no. I got caught with counterfeit money."

The silence on the other end caused his intestines to cramp. "Liz?"

"Wes, don't say another word, not to anyone. Are you still in holding?"

"Yeah."

"Well, the police plant people in holding all the time to get arrestees to talk. Also, your phone calls are monitored. Do you understand what I'm saying?"

"Loud and clear."

"I'll be on the next plane out. Sit tight."

As if he had a choice, Wes thought as he trudged back to holding. When the door opened, he caught a turd on the side of his face.

Perfect.

CHAPTER 14

"I CANNOT BELIEVE you didn't take a picture of your mother," Hannah said, honking at someone who tried to edge in front of her in the evening traffic. As a bonus, she gave them the finger.

"I blanked," Carlotta said. "I was too busy soaking in the news that she's alive, has dementia, and another daughter."

"And now this situation with Wes. How are you even conscious right now?"

"Give me an alternative. My family is in full-blown crisis."

"People check out, turn their backs on their families all the time," Hannah said. "Your parents did."

Her friend was giving her permission to walk away from everything and not feel bad. And didn't some tiny part of her want to? Randolph might be on his death bed, and her mother might not even remember she'd ever been there. But Priscilla would remember, and Carlotta couldn't leave her to the wind, no matter how much the little imp resisted. And she couldn't abandon Wes, not when their family was on the cusp of reuniting.

Or falling apart altogether.

"You don't have to make any decisions tonight," Hannah said. "How bad is your mother?"

"Hard to tell, she went back and forth between current day and the time before she and Randolph left. It was hard to watch her struggle. I got the feeling she knows she's not okay."

"Did you ask her about the evidence your father said he had to exonerate him?"

She nodded. "But either she didn't understand, or she doesn't

103

know."

"Or she wouldn't tell you?"

"That's possible, too," Carlotta said. "She might not trust me." What had Priscilla said? *She doesn't know you.*

"Your mother is awfully young for dementia, isn't she?"

"You would think so. But she's certainly been through a lot—maybe the trauma triggered it."

"Wow, that doesn't bode well for you—" Hannah stopped. "Er, sorry—I shouldn't have said that."

"It's okay. But promise me you won't say anything to anyone about this, especially Chance. I have to find the right time to tell Wes, and while he's under arrest doesn't seem ideal."

"Wonder what the shithead did this time?"

"I don't know. I hope it's something minor, like underage drinking."

"But even something minor will violate his probation, won't it?"

"You're probably right. Maybe Liz can work her magic for him. She seems to have special powers."

"When you spoke to Liz, did she have an update on your dad's condition?"

"No."

"Well, I thought you were cordial to her under the circumstances."

"I haven't been very cordial to Jack."

"That ass-sack deserves whatever you dish out."

"It was nice of him to come out here," Carlotta said. "And to agree to meet me at the police station."

"It's the man's job—he's a cop. It's not like he baked you a cake." Hannah slowed the vehicle and put on the turn signal. "Wow. Guess they don't call this Sin City for nothing—look at the size of that police station."

The massive complex resembled a university more than a jail.

"You can let me off here," Carlotta said, gesturing to a

crosswalk.

"Okay. I'm picking up Chance. If he knows anything about Wes's situation, I'll pass it along."

"Thanks. But remember, not a word about...the other stuff."

Hannah pulled her hand across her mouth in the motion of closing a zipper—which would probably look good on her Goth friend, Carlotta acknowledged.

She climbed out and headed toward the central entrance of the horseshoe-shaped facility, lit up like a tourist attraction. She looked forward to the day when she wasn't familiar with so many different incarceration facilities.

The lobby was jammed with bodies, people standing, sitting, and lying, waiting, she presumed, to see or be seen. A handful of uniformed officers walked around with clipboards answering questions, passing out forms, and generally trying to keep everyone in queues.

Across the teeming room she saw Jack and, God help her, everything was instantly better. He was talking on his phone, but gestured her over. As she approached his tall, muscular form, she snapped the pink elastic bracelet hard against her wrist.

He was putting his phone away when she reached him. "Hi. Another day, a different wig?"

She'd forgotten about the blond wig. "I thought you liked blondes, Jack."

A corner of his mouth went up. "Touché. You look tired."

She wanted to laugh, but didn't have the energy. "It's been a long day, and I guess the time change is getting to me."

He nodded, and his face immediately turned serious.

Her pulse jumped. "What's Wes done now?"

He glanced around. "I was hoping to find somewhere private we could—"

"Just tell me, Jack."

The more he hesitated, the more worried she became. This wasn't an underage drinking charge.

"There are a few charges, but the most serious is placing bets with counterfeit money."

She blinked. "Is this a joke?"

"I'm afraid not. And it's serious, Carlotta."

"We deal with counterfeit money at the mall all the time. Anyone can get a fake twenty in the course of daily transactions— Wes probably didn't even know he had a fake bill."

"It wasn't a fake bill or two. It's over twenty thousand dollars in fake hundreds."

She gasped.

"This is a big-time federal charge, under the jurisdiction of the Secret Service."

She kept breathing, but there didn't seem to be enough oxygen in the room to supply her body, which needed an influx to keep up with this new pinnacle of stress.

She had, it seemed, reached her breaking point.

"Carlotta." Jack's voice sounded distant.

The firm wall of his chest caught her and his arms enveloped her. "I got you," he murmured.

Once she let go of her tears, the floodgate opened—tears for her injured father, tears for her sick mother, tears for her confused little sister, tears for her troubled brother, tears for her compromised heart...tears for her entire broken and bruised family. She leaned into him and heaved great, noisy sobs she'd been holding back for what seemed like most of her adult life. He let her cry for several long minutes, even though she was sure she was causing a scene. When her energy waned, she quieted, drawing on his potency until she felt strong enough to stand on her own. When she pulled away, he had a white handkerchief waiting for her, and the smallest of smiles. "Better?"

She wiped her face and blew her nose, then nodded.

"So it's not good news," he agreed. "But it'll get sorted out."

"Where could he have come into that much money?"

"Not doing anything legal," Jack said.

"His friend Chance is into all kinds of shady stuff, but he's no criminal mastermind. And he has a trust fund, so it's not like he needs money."

Jack pulled his hand over his mouth.

"What?" she asked.

"Do you know if Wes has the skill and equipment to try his hand at printing it himself?"

She touched her temple. "Maybe. He's good at forging event tickets, press passes, things like that to get into places he can't normally access." She pressed her lips together, then said, "He might have created a few gala tickets for me in the past to, um…crash a party or two."

Jack gave her a wry smile. "Imagine that."

"But like I said, that's in the past. And it was tickets to silly cocktail parties, not cash."

"Does he have access to software and sophisticated printers?"

"His probation prohibits him from having computer equipment at home, but he spends a lot of time at Chance's place. And there's his job at the city IT office."

Jack grunted. "Let's hope he wasn't printing it at all, much less on city equipment."

She prayed he wasn't that stupid. "I need to talk to him."

"He's in holding, so let me talk to someone and see if my badge will get us some priority. Will you be okay waiting here?"

She nodded and watched him walk away, pulling her heart along behind him like a battered tin can. She really needed to get over this man and figure out a way to become passionate about her fiancé.

Carlotta pulled out her phone to see a handful of missed texts and calls from Peter. Feeling negligent, she dialed his number, dreading telling him about her latest family fiasco. He answered on the first ring.

"Carly?"

"Hi, Peter."

"Are you okay?"

"Yes, I'm fine."

"You sound like you've been crying. Is it Randolph?"

"No. There's no change in his condition. But I'm at the police station. Wes is in trouble."

He sighed. "What did he do this time?"

"I don't have all the details, but he's been charged with passing counterfeit money—a lot of it."

Peter gave a little laugh. "There has to be a mistake. Where would Wes get counterfeit money?"

"We're trying to get to the bottom of it."

"We?"

"Uh...Jack is here."

"I wish you'd called me instead."

"I thought Jack could help speed things along. He's talking to someone now to see if we can see Wes. After that, I'll come back to the hotel, and maybe you and I can have dinner?"

"I've already eaten. I left you messages."

She winced. "I'm sorry. It's been a crazy day."

"A crazy day of shopping?"

"Um...yeah. Lots of...sales. Maybe we can get dessert when I get back?"

"That would be good," Peter agreed.

"How was your day with clients?"

"Nothing special. We'll talk about it later."

She saw Jack heading back toward her. "I have to go, but I'll be there as soon as I can. Bye." She disconnected the call just as Jack stopped in front of her.

"I tried, but I'm told Wes doesn't want to talk to anyone."

"Even me?" She didn't pretend she didn't feel slighted.

"I'm thinking especially you," Jack said. "But honestly, he's probably just following Liz's instructions, not to talk until she gets here."

"Liz is coming out?"

"So it seems."

"That will make—" Carlotta counted on her fingers. "Eight of us out here. Wow."

Jack winked. "Let's hope eight bodies is enough to get the Wren family back on track."

She was starting to believe that would take an army. "Do you think Wes will be okay here tonight?"

"He'll make it. You're not his mother, Carlotta."

She swung her head up, and her lips parted as the day's revelations washed over her. She ached to tell Jack about the wonder of seeing her mother again, wanted to share with him the heartbreak of her condition, and the surprise of having a baby sister. But she couldn't very well tell Jack the whereabouts of a fugitive and not expect him to act. That would mean guaranteed discharge from the force.

So instead she said, "Old habits die hard, I guess."

He nodded toward the entrance. "Come on—I'll give you a ride back to the hotel and tell you some good news for a change."

"I hope this is about Johnson."

"It is," he said, holding open the door for her to walk through. "And his name was Agent Johns."

"GBI?"

"FBI, actually. Agents Wick and Green grudgingly confirmed he was watching your house in case your mother showed up."

"Doesn't breaking into my hotel room constitute more than just 'watching'?"

He slowed his stride to match hers. "I agree, but when it comes to hunting fugitives, the feds can bend the rules. I guess we'll never know why Johns climbed into the safe but apparently, he had asthma and suffered an attack. His death was ruled natural causes."

"And can I assume the FBI put someone else on my tail?"

"Actually, Wick told me the bureau is standing down."

She hated to hear Johns had died such an untimely death, but at least she didn't have to worry someone would follow her to her mother's. "I'm curious, Jack—what will happen to my mother if she's ever found?"

"She could be prosecuted for aiding and abetting a fugitive, and possibly theft if the D.A. could prove she knew your father had embezzled money and she profited from it. But the real value would be to leverage her in the prosecution of your father."

"You mean threaten to prosecute her if Randolph didn't cooperate?"

"Yes, or threaten to prosecute her to persuade her to turn state's evidence."

"You mean, turn on Randolph?"

"Right."

"What if she...wasn't fit to prosecute?"

Jack stopped by his rental SUV and unlocked the doors. "What do you mean?"

She opened the passenger side door and climbed in. "My mother had a problem with alcohol—she could've gotten worse."

Jack thought it over while he started the engine. "She'd have to be declared incompetent to be excluded. The bar is pretty high for that, though, else every criminal would be claiming they're incompetent to be prosecuted or to testify."

"What happens if my father...doesn't make it?"

Jack's mouth twitched downward. "Chances are, the D.A. will drop the charges."

"Ah—so that's why the feds are standing down? They think Randolph is a dead man."

"I don't know for sure, but I suspect you're right."

"So the only sure way my mother would be safe from prosecution is if my father dies?"

His non-response spoke volumes. "I'm not the person you should be talking to about it. I'm not on the case, remember?"

"Right—sorry. Since the body has been identified and the case closed, I suppose you and Coop are going back to Atlanta."

"Coop is staying to do some hiking." He shifted in his seat. "And since Liz is coming out, I thought I'd stay a few more days."

"Oh," she said to fill in the silence. "That's nice."

"I figure I have a few months to get used to the idea of being a father, and—" He stopped. "I'm sorry, I shouldn't be talking to you about this."

"It's okay, Jack. For what it's worth, I think you'll be a great father."

"That's worth a lot, actually. Thank you."

They were silent during the rest of the ride back to the hotel. Carlotta was churning her thoughts, and it sounded as if Jack has plenty of butter to make, too. The glaring, pulsating lights of Vegas seemed incongruous next to their apprehensions about where life would take them next. The only certainty was it would take them in different directions.

When they got to the hotel and parked, Jack rode up the elevator with her and walked her to her room.

"Thanks again for meeting me at the station," she said.

"You're welcome. Don't worry too much about Wes. He's a big boy."

"I know. And I'm sorry about falling apart back there. I think it's everything piling on."

"No apology necessary. I don't know how you've held up under the pressure as well as you have. And if I've added to that stress load lately, I apologize."

She inclined her head in acceptance.

"So...are we good?" he asked, gesturing between them.

She nodded. "We're good."

The door to the suite opened and Peter stood in the doorway, looking handsome and regal in navy silk pajama pants and a matching robe tied around his waist. "I thought I heard voices."

"Jack and I were just saying good night," Carlotta offered.

Peter curled an arm around her waist protectively. "Thanks, Jack, for seeing Carly back safely."

"No problem," Jack said with a curt nod. "Take care of her, Peter."

"I intend to."

Carlotta watched Jack's receding back for a few seconds, then turned to walk inside with Peter.

CHAPTER 15

"YOU LOOK TERRIBLE, and you smell worse." Liz took out a handkerchief and held it up to her nose and mouth.

Liz Fischer was tall and blond and easy on the eyes, even when her face was tinged with green. "How's the morning sickness?" Wes asked.

"Ongoing," she murmured, sounding stressed. "Look, we don't have much time—your arraignment is in twenty minutes. So let's get to it." She opened a file. "You're being charged with possession of a fake driver's license, underage drinking, possession of counterfeit currency—says here that thirty-two one-hundred-dollar bills were recovered from the lining of your jacket. And last, theft by spending counterfeit currency in and around the hotel casino in the amount of twenty-one thousand dollars." She leveled her gaze on him. "What do you have to say for yourself?"

"That underage drinking charge is totally bogus."

She sighed. "Wes, these are serious federal charges. The good thing is they're non-violent, so if we offer the judge a decent defense, I might get you out on bail, although it could be a substantial amount."

"Don't worry, I have plenty of cash," he joked.

She frowned. "This isn't funny. Where did you get the counterfeit money?"

"I...really can't say."

Her eyes flashed with irritation. "You can say and you *will* say. To me, anyway. Where did you get it?"

If he told her he found it in the wall of the townhome, he'd be implicating his father. Although Randolph had made it clear he didn't want anything to do with him. Wes hated that he still felt compelled to protect the man he could barely remember.

"How's my dad doing?"

"He's slightly better."

"Is he going to make it?"

Her gaze dropped. "It's still touch and go."

He put his hand to his mouth to gnaw his nails. The tips of his fingers were ragged and bloody, but the nasty habit comforted him.

Liz put her beautifully manicured hand over his, pulling it from his mouth. "Look, I know you're worried about your father, but right now you need to be worried about yourself. Where did you get the counterfeit bills?"

"I didn't know they were counterfeit."

"And that will be part of our defense. Possessing counterfeit money isn't as bad as willfully spending it with the knowledge it's fake. But if you tell the Secret Service where you got it and help them take it off the street, that'll go in your favor."

"Even if I got it in an illegal poker game?"

"Yes. But that's not what happened, is it?"

"I didn't print it myself, if that's what you think."

She leaned forward and rubbed her eyes, clearly frustrated. "Good. Because that would be a whole other set of charges. But that's not going to cut it. Now—where did you get the bills?"

When she sat forward like that, her boobs looked huge. He was going to miss seeing those great knockers.

"Wes, if you're protecting someone, it's not worth it, I promise."

She was probably right. If his father died, he wouldn't have to worry about protecting him. But just putting that thought out into the universe made him feel sick.

Besides, the truth might set him free, but Leonard would be waiting for him. He was safer in here, flying shit and all.

She made an exasperated noise. "Wes, I can't help you if you don't tell me where you got the money."

"Don't worry about it, Liz. The time in a cell might do me some good, help me figure out what I'm going to do with my life."

She looked as if she'd like to shake him. "God, you're so much like your father."

And she should know—she'd slept with both of them. "I appreciate you coming all the way out here, Liz. But I don't expect a miracle."

A knock on the door sounded, indicating their consultation time was over.

Wes pushed to his feet.

She reached forward and grasped his hand. "Give me something to tell the Secret Service. Is there more money, or did you spend it all?"

"I'll see you out there."

He walked to the door and turned back. Liz looked distraught, and he felt sorry for being the cause of it. She was only trying to help.

"By the way, Liz...after you told me the kid isn't mine, I never thought to ask. But...who *is* the baby's father?"

"You don't know?"

"Should I?"

"I just assumed you'd heard. It's...Jack Terry."

Wes scoffed. "Really? Wow, okay. I guess that explains why Carlotta has been acting so weird lately."

The guard opened the door. "Time's up."

Liz stood. "You still have time to change your mind, Wes. You should save yourself. Randolph would."

Wes pursed his mouth. "Then maybe I'm not as much like my father as you thought." He turned and walked out, feeling an ounce lighter.

CHAPTER 16

"THAT WAS LIZ," Carlotta said, ending the call.

"How did Wes's arraignment go?" Peter asked.

She sighed. "Not well. He was denied bail."

"That seems harsh."

"Remember he was already on probation. Liz said things would go better for him if he'd tell where he got the money."

"He won't say?"

"He says he got it in an illegal poker game, but even Liz doesn't believe him. The bills are brand new, and sequential."

"So we go back to Atlanta Saturday, and Wes stays here?"

"Looks that way. He'll be in jail until there's a trial."

She swallowed a groan of frustration. She'd been counting on Wes's help if she were able to move their mother and sister to Atlanta. She looked at Peter—she wanted to tell him everything, to be able to rely on him, but she couldn't shake her feeling of distrust after the overheard phone conversation. It had put a wall between them—she could feel him distancing himself from her, too.

"This isn't turning out to be much of a vacation," he said.

She managed a little laugh. "That's an understatement."

"I'm sorry I have to work again today—these clients need more hand-holding than I expected." His mouth curved up, but the smile didn't quite reach his eyes. He seemed on edge this morning, had checked his phone several times.

"You can say it. My father's return has made investors nervous."

"The market's been crazy lately—it doesn't take much to make investors nervous. And Walt's illness hasn't helped. Some of these clients of his have been investing with Mashburn & Tully their entire lives."

"How is Walt?"

"He's, uh, recovering."

Like Randolph, if the reports were to be believed. It was ironic two of the founding partners of the firm were in similar circumstances, albeit on opposite ends of the spectrum where reputation was concerned. The fact that Randolph and Walt had been best friends early in their careers made the situation even more tragic.

"Peter, you once mentioned rumors of a suicide note when Walt overdosed—did you ever hear anything else about it?"

"No. And Walt Tully is such a stand-up guy, I can't see him doing something like that to his family."

His staunch defense of Walt surprised her. Before, Peter had insinuated he hadn't always seen eye to eye with the partners. What had changed?

He checked his phone. "I have to go," he said abruptly, picking up his briefcase. When he reached the door, he turned back. "If you get an update on Randolph's condition, I'd like to know."

"Okay."

The door closed behind him.

"Bye," she murmured.

How many people were monitoring Randolph's condition? And hoping he'd...*die*?

The demise of Randolph "The Bird" Wren would certainly tie up a lot of loose ends. The D.A. in Atlanta could close the case. Her mother could come out of hiding. The tension between her and Peter would be gone. Much of the tension between her and Jack would be gone. Randolph's victims would be relieved. The people who worked at Mashburn & Tully would be relieved.

Heck, maybe Randolph himself would be relieved.

Would she?

It would certainly be nice to wake up in the morning and not feel as if her life was on hold.

But given the choice, she'd rather see her father well and on the run again than to visit him any time she wanted in the cemetery.

"So, dammit, you'd better pull through," she whispered eastward.

Her phoned buzzed with a text from Hannah.

How did Shithead's arraignment go?

Carlotta texted back. *No bail.*

So he happened in Vegas, and he's staying in Vegas?

Wish I could laugh. Wes won't even take my calls.

Sounds like he wants to handle this on his own. You have enough on your plate.

So right. btw, Peter left if you need to use our room to change.

Can't. Since Wes is in jail, I'm babysitting Fat Boy.

You should come out to Chance that you're rich and preppy.

And people in glass houses shouldn't marry Peter Ashford.

Carlotta smirked. Her friend had a point.

A knock sounded at the door. Thinking Peter had forgotten his key, she opened it, surprised to see Jack and Coop standing in the hall.

"Good morning." She crossed her arms over her thin gown. "What's up?"

"Can we talk to you?" Jack asked.

"And Peter," Coop added solicitously.

"Peter left for a meeting, but sure—come in."

When the door closed behind them, she walked over to yank her robe from the unmade bed. Self-consciously she wondered if it was obvious that only the sides of the bed had been mussed, and not the middle.

When she turned back, Jack was looking at the floor, and Coop was studying the ceiling.

"I'm getting a late start this morning," she offered apologetically. "I didn't get much sleep last night."

More shuffling, more gaze averting.

She cleared her throat and gestured to the kitchenette. "Coffee?"

"Sure," they chorused.

She gestured for them to sit, and poured them all a steaming cup. "What's this about?"

Jack sipped from his cup, then nodded to Coop. "Coop is questioning the cause of death of the agent who was following you."

She looked to Coop. "I thought it was an asthma attack."

"Probably," he said. "But I went back the morgue yesterday to help prepare the body to fly back to Atlanta, and I noticed bruising around the neck that wasn't evident in the autopsy. Sometimes bruises are just below the surface and don't fully develop until later, especially if the deceased is sitting up when death occurs. Gravity redistributes the blood."

"Meaning?"

"Meaning," Coop said, "he might've clutched at his own neck during the asthma attack…or he could've been strangled."

Her pulse bumped higher. "You think someone offed the agent who was following me?"

"No," they said in unison.

"But it's possible," Coop added. "Which is why we thought you should know."

"So you don't open your hotel room door when you're alone and half-dressed," Jack said dryly.

She frowned in his direction. "Why would someone strangle the person who's following me? It makes no sense."

"I agree," Jack said, taking another drink from his cup. "But given your penchant for attracting weirdoes, we decided to err on the side of caution."

Coop smiled into his coffee and gave her a wink.

"I told Coop you won't heed the warning, but there—our conscience is clear."

"Gee, thanks."

Jack glanced at his watch. "I have to go. Don't get up, Carlotta. Stay and finish your coffee, Coop." He strode toward the door, then turned back. "By the way—sorry to hear about Wes's arraignment. Liz said if you can get him to tell you where he got the counterfeit bills, things will go more smoothly."

"Easier said than done, but I'll work on it," she promised.

When the door closed, Coop gave her a crooked smile. "So...Wes is in trouble again."

She sipped from her cup. "My little brother seems incapable of behaving himself."

"How did he get his hands on that much counterfeit money?"

"He says he won it in a poker game, but Liz says that doesn't add up. Apparently, the bills are new and the serial numbers are in sequential order."

"You don't think he printed it himself, do you?"

"He says no, but he doesn't seem to have another explanation—not that he's talking to me at all."

Coop made a thoughtful noise. "I knew something was up at the airport. He was as nervous as a cat, and guarding his jacket like it was made of money. I guess it was."

"What on earth was he thinking?"

"He's nineteen. Thinking isn't his strong suit."

She sighed. "The thing is, I really need him right now."

"I heard about your father. You must be worried sick."

She nodded.

"Is there anything I can do to help?"

She started to shake her head, then she smiled. "Actually...do you have plans today?"

"Nothing I can't change."

"Are you up for a top secret field trip?"

"Sounds intriguing."

"I have an old friend who needs a checkup."

He squinted. "A medical checkup?"

"You are a doctor, aren't you?"

Coop laughed. "Yes. But I'm more accustomed to working on people who aren't breathing."

"My friend just needs to know if she's well enough to travel."

"Surely there's someone more appropriate for the job."

"No one she and I can trust."

"Okay. This is getting curiouser and curiouser."

"You can say no."

He gave her a lopsided grin. "And miss out on an adventure? Why would I do that?"

She grinned. "Do you have a rental car?"

"Yeah."

"Meet you at the hotel taxi drop-off in an hour?"

"With bells on."

CHAPTER 17

CARLOTTA PULLED THE RENTAL CAR into the driveway in front of the ranch house in the cookie cutter neighborhood, put the vehicle in park, then cut the engine. "You can look now."

Coop lifted the brim of his fedora to scan his surroundings. "After the ride you just took me on, I wasn't expecting to land in mid-seventies suburbia."

"I took a circuitous route." After hearing Coop's theory that Agent Johns might have been strangled, she wasn't taking any chances of being followed. "Ready?"

He held up a plastic sack. "It's not exactly a physician's black bag, but the pharmacy had instruments to perform a routine exam." He quirked a smile. "I think. It's been a while since I've done one of these."

"Okay, let's go."

When she walked up to the front door, her heart was pounding almost as much as it had been yesterday. She knocked and gave Coop a reassuring glance. He looked alert, but not concerned. She loved how he seemed to take life in stride and with good humor.

Birch opened the door and ushered them inside, glancing out before closing the door. "Hi, Carlotta."

"Hi, Birch. This is Cooper, the doctor friend I told you about on the phone."

The men shook hands and exchanged greetings.

"Melanie is awake," Birch said. "Right this way."

When Carlotta walked into the TV room and saw her mother looking beautiful and serene, she let out a breath she'd been holding. After Hannah had chided her about not taking a picture for proof, Carlotta was half afraid she'd come back and the house would be empty, or someone else would be living there and she'd fantasized the entire thing.

"Melanie, we have company," Birch said.

Her mother lifted her head from the book she was reading and smiled. "Hello."

To Carlotta, her voice sounded like angels singing. "How are you today?"

"I'm just fine," her mother said, then bit into her lip. "Do I know you?"

Carlotta's heart sank in disappointment, but she went to clasp her hand. "We met yesterday. My hair was different. My name is Carlotta."

"Carlotta? What a nice name."

"Thank you. I see you're reading today."

"Yes. It's a very good book." She held up one of the novels Carlotta had bought and shipped to the post office box—but she was reading it upside down.

Carlotta glanced to Coop—he'd noticed.

Her mother looked past her. "And who is this handsome fellow?"

Carlotta smiled and waved him forward. "This is Cooper."

"Well, hello," her mother said, giving him a coy smile.

"Hi, Melanie," Coop said, sandwiching her smaller hand between his two larger ones. "It's nice to meet you."

"Melanie," Birch said, "Cooper is a doctor. He's going to give you a checkup, to make sure you're okay."

She seemed happy about it. "Should I take off my clothes?"

Carlotta gasped.

"That won't be necessary," Coop said, not missing a beat. "Is it alright if I move this chair closer to you?"

"Of course. We won't tell my husband."

Carlotta exchanged wide-eyed glances with Birch.

"I won't tell if you won't," Coop said with a smile. He put a stethoscope around his neck. "I'm going to listen to your heart first."

"You're making it beat very fast," her mother said, batting her eyelashes.

Biting back a smile, Carlotta stood at the rear of room with Birch as Coop took her blood pressure, looked into her ears and eyes, and checked her reflexes.

Carlotta took the opportunity to snap a couple of photographs of her mother. "I saw you checking outside when we came in," she said to Birch. "Is everything okay?"

Birch nodded. "I'm just being careful after your warning. Is there anything you can tell me about the people who might come looking for Melanie?"

She shook her head. "I'm sorry. I wish I could be more specific. In a few more days I should know more about Randolph's situation."

"Your visit triggered a lot of memories," Birch murmured. "She's been talking nonstop about Mr. Randolph."

"It made Mommy sad," Priscilla said.

Carlotta turned to see the little girl standing in the doorway wearing a red dress and a black frown. "Hi, Priscilla. I thought you'd be in school today."

"We're on break," she said glumly. "Dad promised he would take me to the Eiffel Tower."

"He was going to take you to Paris on your school break?"

Priscilla rolled her eyes. "No. To the Eiffel Tower Experience downtown."

"Oh, right. I remember seeing a brochure about it in the hotel."

"Do you know when he's coming home?"

"I'm sorry, I don't. But I'm sure he misses you."

"Of course he misses me," the girl said in a haughty tone.

"Who is this?" Coop asked, walking up.

"This is Priscilla," Birch said, "the head of the household."

"I can see that," Coop said. "Hi, Priscilla, I'm Cooper."

"Why are you giving those tests to my mother?"

"Just to make sure she's okay."

"But she's not okay. Can you make her okay?"

Carlotta's heart squeezed at the girl's pleading tone.

"I'm not that kind of doctor," Coop said gently. "But there might be doctors out there who can make her some better."

"Can you help us find one?" the girl asked.

"I will try," Coop said, giving her a wink.

That got a shy smile out of her, revealing the telltale gap between her front teeth. Coop looked back and forth between Carlotta and Priscilla, then turned toward Birch. "How long has Melanie had memory issues?"

"She was like this when I came to work for the family two years ago."

"During that time has her memory or motor skills gotten worse?"

"Not really. I kept expecting her to, but she's been pretty much the same."

Coop squatted down to be on Priscilla's level. "Do you remember when your mother started forgetting things?"

She nodded. "She forgot my sixth birthday."

"And how old are you now?"

"I'm nine."

"Okay, that helps," Coop said.

"All done?" Carlotta asked.

Coop nodded. "Do you have her medical records?"

"Some," Birch said, reaching for a manila file on an end table. "I made a copy for you, including her medications."

"Thank you," Carlotta said. "We'll go. I'll call you later." Then she turned to Priscilla. "I know it's not the same, but how about I come back tomorrow to take you to the Eiffel Tower? If that's okay with Birch?"

He nodded.

Despite her taciturn mood, the little girl couldn't help but look excited. "I guess that would be okay."

Carlotta was happy to see a crack in the little girl's veneer. "Okay, I'll see you tomorrow."

She went back to her mother's chair. Valerie had resumed "reading" the book, but she was simply turning the pages. Her heart squeezed at the look of concentration on her mother's face.

"Goodbye for now," Carlotta said. "I'll see you again tomorrow."

"Okay, dear. If you see Wesley outside riding his bike, will you tell him to come inside? I'll have dinner ready soon."

Carlotta pressed her lips together. "Yes, of course I'll tell him. Goodbye."

"Goodbye."

She walked to the door with Coop and out into the sunshine. He was silent until they climbed in the car and she'd backed the rental car out of the driveway.

"Is that who I think it is?" Coop asked.

She threaded their way through the maze of identical streets. "I wouldn't want you to know anything that would put you at odds with the fugitive task force. Or Jack Terry."

He dipped his chin in concession. "And the girl?"

"An unexpected bonus," Carlotta said with a smile. "What's your assessment of Melanie's medical condition?"

He was reviewing her medical records. "According to this file, the doctor she sees is treating her for Alzheimer's, although it's not immediately clear what tests she's undergone. There are different forms of dementia, but I'm not remotely qualified to make a diagnosis."

"Do you think she's well enough to travel?"

"In my opinion, yes. Her vital signs are strong, and her motor skills are good. You might ask her caretaker if she has anxiety around crowds or in confined spaces. But physically, she seems healthy."

She smiled. "How can I thank you?"

"Not necessary. I'm happy to help. How did you find this, uh, *friend* of yours?"

"I came into possession of a post office box address, and followed it from there."

"Hm. Jack said the address on the piece of paper in the mouth of Agent Johns was a P.O. box business."

She nodded. "I ran into Jack there. He accused me of taking the piece of paper out of the agent's mouth and putting it back, but I didn't—I already had the address. I don't know how the agent got it, but I have a theory about why it was in his mouth when he died."

"Lay it on me."

"If you had an address written on a sticky note that could lead to the whereabouts of a fugitive, and someone you didn't want to have it confronted you, what would you do with the note?"

Coop looked over at her. "I'd eat it."

"So would I."

Coop pulled his hand over his mouth. "Now I understand the subterfuge. Who else knows about this house?"

"Hannah was with me when I staked out the post office box and followed Birch here. Counting you that makes two."

"Not even Peter?"

She shook her head and tightened her grip on the steering wheel. Especially not Peter.

CHAPTER 18

"WE HAVE TO DO SOMETHING." Peter's voice reverberated low and agitated.

Carlotta stood in the dark around the corner from his dressing room, listening to his phone conversation. She couldn't tell who he was talking to, but he sounded desperate.

"I'm trying to stay calm, but we're running out of time."

The sheer panic in his words stirred the tiny hairs on the nape of her neck. She had awoken to find his side of the bed empty, and followed the glow of his phone.

"If you don't pull the trigger tomorrow," he warned, "I'll do it myself."

Sensing the end of the conversation, she crept back to her side of the bed and feigned sleep when Peter came back to the main room. He went to the kitchenette and poured something in a glass, then stood by the window looking at the lights of the city, his shoulders bowed as if the weight of the world were on them. She lay there tingling in the dark, trying to remember her optimism when she'd thought Vegas could be a place for them to start over. Instead, they each seemed to have found more problems to distract them from each other.

The last time she'd seen Peter this out of sorts, he'd confessed to his wife Angela's murder. Only she had believed him innocent despite the evidence to the contrary.

She wanted to think the best of him again, and she truly believed Peter would never hurt her physically, but she was worried this time whatever he was involved with was bound up in her family somehow.

Every path she took seemed to lead back to Randolph.

She must have fallen asleep because the next time she opened her eyes, daylight streamed into the room and Peter's side of the bed was cold. He'd left her a note saying he would try to be back to the hotel this evening in time for them to have dinner together. He signed it with "I love you. Always, Peter."

Bittersweetness welled up in her chest. Was it possible she and Peter liked the idea of being a couple more than actually being a couple?

She retrieved her phone and unlocked the screen, hating that she'd gotten into the habit of putting safeguards on her device. As soon as she got back to Atlanta, she was buying a new phone with her own service plan.

Priscilla would probably need some sort of phone, too. Not something fancy enough to stream porn and other objectionable material—like discount shopping ads—but a model that would allow her to contact Carlotta anytime, anyplace.

And just like that, she realized she'd already made room for the little girl in her heart. Once they got home, Coop would help her find a doctor for Valerie, and they'd sort things out.

The big question mark was if Randolph would be there...or alive.

She texted Liz. *Any news on Randolph's condition?*

Same, holding. Have you convinced Wes to talk about the money?

No, will try again today.

Try hard.

Carlotta frowned. She appreciated Liz helping Wes, but the woman didn't have to act as if she was the only one who cared about her brother's welfare. Although, maybe it was Liz's way to make up for the baby-daddy debacle. And she was probably eager for her client to avoid a trial about the time Liz would be very pregnant.

With Jack, Jr.

She snapped the pink bracelet on her abused wrist and consoled herself with the knowledge that as the bruise worsened, her heart was healing.

After pouring herself a cup of coffee, she moved to the window to take in the frantic display—was neon really necessary before noon?—and called Hannah.

"Hiya. What's up?"

"I was wondering if Chance had been to see Wes."

"No. He's talked to him on the phone a couple of times."

"At least Wes is talking to someone. Is he okay?"

"Chance said he's holding up."

"Does Chance know where Wes got the counterfeit money?"

"He told Chance he won it in a poker game."

So he was still standing by his original story. "Okay, thanks. Also, I was hoping I could borrow your rental car today if you're not using it."

"Are you going to see you-know-who?"

Carlotta frowned. "Yes."

"Want some company?"

"Uh—actually, I'm taking Priscilla on an outing—you know, just the two of us."

"So Coop gets an introduction to your new family, and I don't?"

Carlotta blinked at Hannah's hurt tone. "It's not like that. I want you to meet them when the time is right."

"Well, actually, I'm going to need the rental car today."

Her friends sounded...*angry*? "No problem," Carlotta said lightly. "I'll get a car. Maybe we can have a drink when I get back?"

"Um...I'm going to be busy."

"Okay. Hopefully I'll see you tomorrow."

"Yeah, sure. Listen, I have to go."

"Bye," Carlotta said, but Hannah had already disconnected the call.

She chalked up the strange behavior to Hannah's anxiety over revealing her other persona to Chance. But the fact that Hannah and Chance were together to begin with still boggled her mind.

With Coop's theory about the dead agent still in mind, she walked to a rental car place, keeping an eye out for anyone following her. After securing a mid-size sedan, she decided to first drive to the jail to try to talk to Wes.

After the ordeal of parking and waiting to request to see him, she was told he'd refused to see her. She left a care package of candy bars and a science fiction novel she found in the gift shop. Inside the front cover of the book she wrote. *I need to see you before I leave LV. Very important. Love, C*

She left the jail and drove a winding path back to the little ranch house, with one eye on the rearview mirror. At one point she noticed a green car hanging back several hundred yards, but she made a few turns into the labyrinth of subdivisions and didn't see it again. By the time she pulled onto the driveway where Melanie and Priscilla lived, she conceded her father had chosen a good place to hide his family. The neighborhood was numbingly unvaried. If not for the house numbers, it would be nearly impossible to tell one home from the one next to it. They were all within a few paint shades of adobe, all with tumbled rock lawns instead of grass in deference to the desert heat, all with the same sago palm tree and scrub bushes for landscaping. As long as the residents didn't do anything to stand out, they could probably go relatively unnoticed.

But this was no life for a child.

When Carlotta knocked on the front door, Priscilla opened it, with Birch close behind.

"Are you ready?" Carlotta asked.

"Yes," the girl said primly, her eyes wide. "I put on lots of sunscreen."

Birch told her to have a good time and mind her manners. And Carlotta noticed she skipped a little on the way to the car. She was wearing purple shorts and a flowered T-shirt, with white sandals. Once inside the rental, Priscilla fastened her seatbelt with precision and sat in the seat like a little soldier.

"I like your outfit," Carlotta said.

"Thank you. I like pretty clothes."

Carlotta laughed. "So do I. In fact, I work at a department store."

"You do?"

"Uh-huh. In a mall." Carlotta backed the car out of the driveway and headed toward the Strip.

"Do you have kids?"

"No. I'm not married."

"You don't have to be married to have kids."

Out of the mouth of babes. "That's true."

"Where is my daddy?"

"He's in Atlanta. He's...sick."

"Sick like Mom?"

"Uh, no. He...fell and hurt himself."

"Is he going to get better?"

"I hope so."

She turned big brown eyes toward Carlotta. "Who's going to take care of us?"

Carlotta swallowed hard. "I am."

"We're going to live with you in Atlanta?"

"Would you like that?"

"I don't know," the girl said, looking earnest. "Can I think about it?"

"Of course. Why don't you tell me about school?"

Carlotta listened to her chatter about her friends and teachers and subjects she liked while looking out for the green car, but she didn't see it again.

The Eiffel Tower Experience was connected to the Paris hotel on the Strip, over the casino. The tower itself was a half scale model of the world-famous landmark, but since she'd never been to Paris, to Carlotta it was as breathtaking as the real thing. They strolled along the base of the tower with other tourists, eating ice cream and gazing up through the steel structure. Since Priscilla had been many times, Carlotta let her be the tour guide. When she wasn't conscious of having to be quiet and deferential to her mother, the little girl was gregarious and outgoing. Yet when they had to walk through the colorful casino to get to the entrance of the attraction, she shied away from the crush of strangers and the loud clanging of the gambling machines, and reached for Carlotta's hand.

Carlotta was careful not to make a big deal out of it, but she was shot through with love for the little girl, and angry all over again that their parents had kept the siblings apart.

She purchased tickets to the observation tower in the gift shop, then they rode up a glass elevator forty-six stories to the top. Priscilla led her all around the three hundred sixty-degree tower, pointing out landmarks and eagerly awaiting the regular Bellagio fountain show that ran every thirty minutes. While they waited for the show to begin, they people-watched. Tourists came in every shape and size, and no matter the age, everyone seemed enthralled by the simple act of being higher than everything else around them.

Priscilla pointed to a bride and groom who were walking around the tower deck in full regalia, accepting congratulations from strangers.

"Do you like her dress?" Carlotta asked.

"It's a little fussy for my tastes," Priscilla said. "But it suits her."

Carlotta laughed. "We're going to get along fine."

They turned back to reclaim their viewing spot.

And came face to face with Jack Terry and Liz Fischer.

CHAPTER 19

"COME ON, MAN. Two Snickers bars for one lousy phone call on your cell." Wes wagged the candy bars in front of the chubby guard. Carlotta's care package had given him some trading currency.

"That's against the rules, dude."

"I need to call my probation officer back in Atlanta and check in. If the Clark County Jail shows up on her caller ID, I'm screwed."

"She's gonna find out about your arrest eventually."

"I'm just trying to buy a little time, that's all. Who's gonna know?"

The guy looked all around, then grabbed the candy bars and handed over his phone. "Make it quick."

Wes punched in the number and waited.

"Atlanta Department of Community Supervision. How may I direct your call?"

"Eldora Jones, please," he said in his most authoritative voice.

"Who should I say is calling?"

"Wesley Wren. Tell her it's important."

A few seconds later, E.'s voice came on the line. "Hey, Wes. How's Vegas?"

"It's good," he said cheerfully. "I told you I'd call to check in, so…I'm calling to check in."

"Staying out of trouble, I hope?"

"You know it."

"Good. I hear the weather is nice."

"Yeah. How'd you hear that?"

"It's so bizarre. Leonard's in Vegas, too."

His stomach fell to his shins. "You don't say?" He swallowed. "Why didn't you come with him?"

"It was a last-minute work thing. But maybe we'll honeymoon there."

Wes surveyed the dried booger someone had wiped on the cell wall. "Yeah, Vegas is a real romantic place. How long is Leonard staying?"

"He isn't sure, says he has to stay until the job is done."

"Bummer," he muttered.

"Thanks for checking in, Wes. I'll see you when you get back in town."

"Okey-dokey." He ended the call and pulled his hand down his face. He was a dead man. He let the realization sink in for a few seconds, then punched in Meg's number.

"Hey, you said one call," the guard sputtered through a mouthful of chocolate.

"Five minutes," Wes said, then extended a Milky Way through the bars.

The guy snatched it. "Two minutes."

He was planning to leave a voice message, but to his surprise, she answered.

"This is Meg."

"Hi...it's Wes."

"This isn't your number."

"Lost my phone," he lied.

"Ah. Well, when I saw it was a Vegas number I thought it might be you calling."

He grinned. "You did?"

"Yeah. I miss you a little bit."

He grinned wider. "You do?"

"Don't let it go to your head. I miss RadioShack, too, and it wasn't so great."

He leaned back against the bars. "So you like the bracelet, huh?"

"Yeah. It's nice."

"Nice enough for a second chance?"

"Hm…we'll see. Don't get your hopes up."

"I won't."

"When do you get back?"

"Soon," he lied.

"Maybe I'll see you."

"Yeah, maybe."

"Gotta run," she said. "But I'm glad you called. Put a quarter in a slot machine for me."

"I will," he said. "Bye."

Wes ended the call and handed the phone back to the guard. "Thanks, man."

"That must've been some phone call. You look drunk."

"I have a date. With a girl I'm crazy about."

The man scoffed. "A date? You're not getting out of here, Money Man."

Wes sighed. "Yeah, there's that." And if he ever did, Leonard would be waiting for him.

CHAPTER 20

JACK AND LIZ SEEMED as taken aback as Carlotta, and for a few seconds, everyone froze.

Liz recovered first. "Carlotta...what a surprise."

"Hi, Liz...Jack."

"Hi, Carlotta," he said, looking pretty uncomfortable considering he was dressed down in jeans and black T-shirt. Liz was dressed casually, too, in a dress that emphasized her growing baby bump. Jack's gaze immediately went to Priscilla. "Who's this?"

"I'm Priscilla," the girl said, staring up at Jack with a look Carlotta recognized as pure female fascination.

"Priscilla is a friend," Carlotta said quickly. "The daughter of a friend, actually."

"Nice to meet you, Priscilla. I'm Jack, and this is Liz."

"Hello," Liz said with a tentative smile, as if she were afraid Priscilla would bite.

"Are you a lumberjack?" Priscilla asked Jack.

He squatted down to be on her level. "No. I'm a policeman."

"Can I see your badge?"

He chuckled, then pulled out his wallet and showed her his shield.

"Wow," she breathed.

He opened his wallet and pulled out a sticker of a gold shield with space for a name. "You can have this if you like."

She nodded happily.

He pulled a pen out of his pocket. "How do you spell your name?"

"You can call me 'Prissy.' P-R-I-S-S-Y."

The little flirt. But the girl seemed to have found an admirer in Jack. Carlotta was fascinated to see him interact with a child, and was surprised how much at ease he seemed.

He wrote Prissy's name in block letters and handed the sticker to her.

"Thank you," she said with a gap-toothed grin.

Carlotta knew the instant Jack recognized the telltale family trait. He pushed to his feet and gave Carlotta a questioning look, but she pretended not to notice.

"Carlotta," Liz said, "have you had a chance to talk to Wesley?"

"I tried today. *Hard,*" she added, referencing Liz's text. "But he wouldn't see me."

"Are you having a baby?" Priscilla blurted, staring at Liz's stomach.

"Yes, I am."

"Is it a boy or a girl?"

"Actually," Liz said, smiling up at Jack, "it's a boy. We just found out."

A zing of envy barbed though Carlotta's chest, but she kept smiling. "Congratulations," she said, and found she meant it. Jack would love having a boy.

He inclined his head in thanks.

"Are you two married?" Priscilla asked.

Carlotta winced inwardly. But she had to admit it was a little satisfying to see Jack squirm.

"No," he said. "We're not married."

Priscilla looked up at Carlotta. "See? I told you, you don't have to be married to have a baby."

"Yes, you did," Carlotta said with a little smile.

"Why don't you get married here?" Priscilla suggested, then

pointed to the bride and groom a few yards away. "They did."

Liz's smile was getting tighter and tighter, and Jack looked as if he might take a flying leap from the tower.

"That's enough," Carlotta said, shushing her.

But Priscilla ignored her, taking a step toward Jack. *"I'll* marry you."

Carlotta pursed her mouth. Liz gave a nervous little laugh. Jack reached over and touched the tip of Priscilla's nose. "Then I'll save myself for you."

"The fountain show is starting," Carlotta said to Priscilla, gesturing to the viewing portholes. At last the spell was broken, and she ran over to watch.

Liz pointed to her phone. "Sorry, I need to make a quick call." She stepped a few feet away and left Carlotta and Jack standing alone.

"Cute kid," he said, nodding toward Priscilla.

"She's a little precocious. Sorry if she embarrassed you."

"Sometimes I think we'd all be better off if we were as honest as kids are. But I think the older we get, the better we are at...hiding things."

She realized he was waiting for a response, so she shrugged. "If you say so, Jack."

She saw Liz coming back, so she gave a wave, then went to stand behind Priscilla. When she looked back a few minutes later, the couple was gone. Carlotta exhaled in relief. Things could've really gone sideways.

"Where did your friends go?" Priscilla asked after the show.

"They had to leave."

"I liked Jack."

"Most women do," she murmured. "Are you ready to ride back down?"

Priscilla nodded, and they waited for the next empty elevator. The ride down was just as thrilling as the ride up, maybe even more of a rush. When they got to the ground, Carlotta walked off a little unsteadily, making her little sister laugh.

"Can we get our picture taken?" Priscilla asked, pointing to a photo booth in the lobby.

"That sounds fun," Carlotta agreed. They went into the booth and crowded together on the bench. She fed money into the machine, then they mugged for the camera, making funny faces between flashes.

"I like your bracelet," Priscilla said, touching the pink beads.

Carlotta smiled. "Then it's yours." She slid the bracelet off her wrist and put it on Priscilla's.

"Are you sure?" Priscilla asked.

"Yes. Actually, I don't need it anymore."

"Thank you," Priscilla said, then threw her arms around Carlotta's neck in an unexpected hug. "I'm glad you came for us."

Carlotta swallowed a lump in her throat. "So am I."

They came out of the booth and when the machine spit out the strip of photos, they laughed. Carlotta tore the strip to divide the pictures. "Two for me, and two for you. Are you hungry?"

"Starved," Priscilla said dramatically.

They walked down the Strip and bought messy hotdogs to eat. Carlotta was happy to see her little sister having fun. She got the feeling it didn't happen often, but she vowed to change that.

When she was tossing the trash, she spotted two more familiar faces—the would-be thieves from the restaurant and the coffee shop. One of them spotted her at the same time and elbowed his friend. She wasn't wearing the enormous diamond ring, but they couldn't tell at this distance. They headed in her direction.

"Come on, Priscilla, let's go this way." She turned abruptly and almost mowed down a man walking behind her.

"Sorry," she said, then squinted.

She recognized him, too, but she couldn't remember where she'd met him. A skullcap covered his hair, but the eyebrows and sideburns were dark, and his features were distinctive. She could tell from the look on his face that he also knew her. But he untangled himself and kept going. As she watched, he looked back, then began to jog away.

She looked down to see he'd dropped a set of keys for a rental car. She scooped them up just as she remembered where she'd met him—he was the fiancé of Eldora Jones, Wes's probation officer. She'd met him once at the Fox Theater, and she'd talked to Eldora just recently at a wedding expo.

"Leonard," she called, waving. "You dropped your keys. Leonard!" Then she gasped. "Look out!"

He was looking back at her, still jogging. She watched in slow-motion horror as he stepped into the path of a bus. She turned to shield Priscilla's face and ears from the sight and the sickening thud of the body landing. Gasps sounded, then screams.

Carlotta pressed Priscilla's face against her stomach. "Don't look back. Don't look back."

But Carlotta could see, and from the look of the man's twisted body, she knew he wouldn't be getting up. She saw Jack and Liz emerge from the crowd and move toward the scene. Jack waved people back and Liz was on her phone, presumably calling 9-1-1.

Her mind raced—how odd that someone else from Atlanta would be here, in the same public place, mere steps behind her...and when she called him by name, he would literally run from her?

She looked at the keys she was holding and on impulse, held them up and depressed the panic button on the keyless remote. Across the street just beyond the bus crash, a car's lights started flashing and the horn blaring.

A green car.

"Come on," she murmured to Priscilla. "Time to go." She turned and led her in the opposite direction. As they walked past a storm drain, she tossed the rental keys inside.

On the drive back to the house, she tried to distract Priscilla and lighten the mood by stopping to get an ice cream cake to take back to her mother and Birch and joking with her about boy bands she liked. Even though she knew the man who'd been following her was no more, she occasionally glanced in the side mirror, and her heartrate remained elevated. How close had the man come to finding her mother? And how gut-wrenching to know she was the one who'd almost led him to the door.

"Did that man back there die?" Priscilla asked, proof she, too, was still thinking about what had happened.

"I don't know, sweetie, but it looked like a bad accident."

"Did you know him?"

"No. I thought I did, but I was mistaken."

She seemed to accept the explanation and happily launched into an earnest discussion about her favorite movies. Carlotta realized she was going to have to get up to speed on superheroes and princesses.

When they pulled into the driveway, it was late afternoon. Carlotta let Priscilla carry the cake. While they waited for Birch to open the door, they heard the sound of a car stopping in front of the house.

Priscilla turned and grinned. "Jack!"

CHAPTER 21

CARLOTTA UTTERED a silent curse and took her time turning around.

Thankfully, Jack was alone, walking toward them with long, confident strides. He had donned a jacket, she knew, to conceal his sidearm. She couldn't tell by looking at him what frame of mind he was in, but he wasn't smiling.

"Hi, Prissy," he said. "Carlotta."

"Hi, Jack. Are you following me?"

"When it's police work, we call it surveillance."

The door opened and Birch warily studied Jack.

"Why don't you take the cake inside with Birch, sweetie?" Carlotta urged Priscilla.

"Okay. Jack, are you going to have cake with us?"

"We'll see," he said with a wink.

"It's okay," Carlotta said to Birch. "Give me a minute."

When the door closed, Jack said, "I saw you at the site of the bus accident."

"Is the man dead?"

He nodded. "Leonard Motts, from Atlanta. No rap sheet, but reported connections to some bad people, including Hollis Carver."

"The loan shark?"

He nodded. "Motts got into town Saturday, just before you and Peter. I found a keycard in his wallet from your hotel, and I'm betting it opens the door to the room Agent Johns died in."

She swallowed hard. "Okay."

"So, what's behind this door that everyone is so interested in finding, and you're so interested in hiding?"

"I think you know the answer to that," she said softly. "So if you're here doing police work, you should leave...for your own sake and for mine."

He looked away, then shifted his weight and looked back. "What if I'm here as a friend?"

Carlotta smiled and reached for the doorknob. "Then come in."

She stepped inside the house and Jack followed. His head was on a pivot, scanning and recording, as she knew was his second nature. They followed voices into the kitchen where Priscilla, Birch, and her mother sat around a table eating slices of the ice cream cake. Jack and Birch traded nods.

Valerie looked up. "Hello there."

"Hi, Mom," Carlotta said, then leaned forward to kiss Valerie's cheek. "How are you today?"

"I'm wonderful, look at this beautiful cake."

"I see. Mom, I want you to meet a friend of mine. This is Jack."

Her mother smiled up at Jack. "Oh, you're a tall one, like my husband Randolph."

"Yes," Jack said. "I've met your husband."

Valerie frowned. "He's working late again. He's at that office all the time. They make a lot of money there." She took another bite of the cake on her plate and chewed happily. "But he brings me those paper things, oh, what are they called?"

"Books?" Carlotta supplied.

"That's right—books," Valerie said, then she angled her head at Carlotta. "Do I know you?"

"Yes. We've met before. My name is Carlotta."

"Oh, my daughter's name is Carlotta." Valerie looked at Priscilla. "Carlotta, say hello to this nice young woman. Her name is also..." She looked back to Carlotta and her eyes dimmed, then she took another bite of cake. "Randolph and I are thinking about having another baby, and if it's a boy, we'll name him Wesley."

"Wesley is a wonderful name," Carlotta agreed. She swung her gaze up to Jack. His expression was unreadable.

"Jack, do you want a piece of cake?" Priscilla asked.

"Not this time, Prissy. Next time, I promise."

"Mom," Priscilla said, "I'm going to marry Jack."

Valerie laughed merrily. "Oh, Carlotta, you're not going to marry Jack. You're going to marry..." She stopped, then shrugged. "Someone else."

Carlotta pressed her lips together. How true.

"I'm going to let you all enjoy your cake," Jack said. "Bye, everyone."

"I'll walk you out," Carlotta said.

When they got to the door, he made an anguished noise. "I'm so sorry about your mother. You finally find her, and now..."

"I know. But it also explains a lot."

"Priscilla is your sister, I assume?"

She nodded. "I'm guessing Valerie was pregnant when they left."

"Wow."

"What are you going to do, Jack?"

"What are *you* going to do?"

"Wait to see if Randolph recovers...or not. If he doesn't recover, then I can bring Mom out of hiding. If he does, then I hope the D.A. and all the victims recognize she doesn't pose a threat to anyone."

Jack pulled on his chin. "But if Randolph is in custody, why would someone be trying to get to your mom?"

"Randolph told me he had evidence that would exonerate him. I think someone else knows what that evidence is, and they believe my mother knows, too, and that she might be keeping it safe for him."

Jack frowned. "Wait—when did you talk to your father?"

She winced. "Hannah and I sort of broke into the prison, and I got to talk to him for, like, a minute."

His mouth opened, but no sound came out for a full ten seconds. "You and Hannah broke into the federal penitentiary?"

"'Broke into' is probably the wrong phrase. More like, smuggled ourselves in."

A vein bulged in his neck. "Really? You're debating semantics?" He pressed his palms into his eyes and made a strangled noise. "I can't know about this, any of this."

"What are you saying, Jack?"

"I'm saying I was never here."

She smiled. "Thanks, Jack."

"Don't—" His mouth tightened, then he opened the door and walked out.

Carlotta closed the door, smiled to herself, then backtracked to the kitchen to have a piece of cake.

"Was that Randolph at the door?" Valerie asked.

"No, Mom. He's away," Carlotta said.

"Oh, that's right."

"Before he left, did Dad give you anything to keep for him?" she asked, thinking this time, Valerie might remember more.

"Oh, just those paper things," Valerie said. "He's always bringing home those paper things."

"Right," Carlotta said. "Books." She ate another bite of cake and glanced around the kitchen. "Does the door lead to a backyard?"

"A small one," Birch said. "But we have to keep the door deadbolted to prevent Melanie from...traveling."

Carlotta nodded. Good to know for the future. She gestured to the doggie door. "You have a dog?"

"No," Priscilla said glumly, then her eyes lit up. "But I'd like one."

Hm—also good to know for the future.

"The previous owners must've had a dog," Birch said. "But

we've got our hands full around here, already, don't we, Prissy?"

Priscilla nodded, and Carlotta felt another pang for the girl's missed childhood. Still, overall, she seemed well-adjusted and bright. She chatted about the views from the Eiffel Tower Experience, and the bride and groom on the observation deck.

"Then we saw a man get run over by a bus," Priscilla said.

Birch sent a worried look to Carlotta.

"There was an accident—a man ran out in the road. But thank goodness we were far enough away that we didn't see anything bad."

"Is he dead?" Valerie asked.

"I don't think this is table conversation," Birch said gently.

"Why?" Valerie asked. "People die all the time. Good people, bad people. They were going to kill us, you know…that's why we had to leave town." She choked. "That's why we had to leave our children."

Carlotta reached for her mother's hand. "Who were you afraid of, Mom? Who was going to hurt you?"

"Those bad men. You know."

"Tell me their names."

Valerie sat there shaking her head, rocking forward and backward.

Carlotta stroked her hand to calm her. "It's okay, Mom. The bad men aren't here."

Valerie turned to her and smiled. "Do I know you?"

Carlotta smiled back. "Yes, we've met. My name is Carlotta."

"Such a pretty name," her mother said. "My daughter's name is Carlotta."

"Look, Mom." Priscilla held up the picture of her and Carlotta together, flashing identical gapped grins.

Valerie gasped. "You two look so much alike, you could be sisters."

They were quiet for a few seconds, then they all burst out

laughing.

But later when she walked into the empty hotel room, Carlotta felt raw and drained. The scene of Leonard stepping in front of the bus kept replaying in her head.

When she assisted Coop on body-moving runs, they dealt with bodies after the violent end. The mechanics of death neutralized dying, made it seem more peaceful than it was. But to see a man alive one second, and dead the next had been a shock to her system. And made her feel lucky to be alive.

When she stepped into the palatial shower, it seemed as if every sense was heightened—the fall of the water on her skin, the scent of the luxurious vanilla soap, the sound of the splash against the porcelain tiles.

When she heard a noise, she turned around, startled to see a figure moving slowly toward her. Then she realized it was Peter, fully dressed, his tie loose and shoulders slumped, as if he'd had a day similar to hers.

He opened the door of the shower and leaned on the frame, unabashedly watching her. He'd seen her naked many times. He'd been her first lover when she was a teenager. And since they'd reunited, they'd attempted to make love a few times. But she'd never seen this look of raw hunger before.

She liked it.

She went to him and looped her arms around his neck, raising her mouth for a kiss. He slanted his lips over hers with an unfamiliar intensity. He pulled her wet body against the coarse fabric of his suit, running his hands down her back and cupping her to him. She arched into him, feeling loose and languid against his hardness.

With a groan he picked her up and carried her to the bed, splashing a trail behind them. When the cool air hit her wet body, her breasts and shoulders and thighs came alive. Peter shed his jacket and unfastened his pants, then climbed on top of her.

"I want you, Carly," he whispered in her ear. "I want you so much."

"I want you, too, Peter. Take me."

She opened her knees to him, and he thrust into her with a force that shook her. He found a feverish rhythm, driving deeper each stroke, until she clawed at his back and gasped her release. With a fierce plunge, he took his own guttural release, as if he were pouring everything he had left into her.

The sex left her utterly satiated, but with a sense of foreboding that things between her and Peter had reached some sort of pinnacle they would never be able to replicate.

CHAPTER 22

"WREN, YOU GOT A VISITOR."

Wes looked up from the game of solitaire he was playing on his cot. "Who is it?"

"Do I look like your personal secretary?"

"Man, woman?"

"Says she's one of your sisters."

"I only have one sister."

"Also says she's not going to feed your pet snake unless you talk to her."

Wes grimaced. He'd forgotten about Einstein. The black and gray spotted axanthic ball python rarely ate—he suspected it was vegetarian. But if this jail spa retreat of his lasted longer than a couple of weeks, it would need some nourishment.

"Uncle," he muttered and trudged to the visitation room.

Carlotta sat at a table staring at something in her hand. When she saw him, she jumped up to hug him.

"No contact," the guard said.

She sighed, but refrained and sat back down. "Hi, Wes."

"Hi, yourself. How's Dad?"

"Improving, slowly."

"That's good to hear. I guess."

"Why have you been avoiding me?"

Because he didn't want to see how disappointed she was in him. Again. "I didn't want you to get involved. I messed up. This is all on me."

"Where did you get the counterfeit money, Wes?"

"At a poker club in Atlanta. It was a pot I won."

"I'm told that's probably not true."

He chewed on his lower lip. "What if I said I found it?"

"I'd ask where."

He nodded to the piece of paper she had curled in her hand. "What's that?"

"Something *I* found, actually."

"What?"

She handed him a picture of a woman with graying hair. Something about her...

His head came up. *"Mom?"*

She nodded, smiling.

His pulse skyrocketed. "Really? How? Have you seen her? Did she come looking for Dad?"

"I found her. She's here in Vegas. And we have a baby sister, she's nine."

Wonder flooded his chest. "How did you find them?"

"It's a long story, but basically, I found out where Randolph was monitoring the listening device from. You were right about it being a house—it was our old house in Buckhead."

"Seriously?"

She nodded. "He bought the house under a different name a few months ago. I went inside and found a receipt for a post office box here in Vegas, and I suspected Mom was here."

"That's why you wanted to come to Vegas?"

"Other reasons, too."

"Yeah, Liz told me Jack is her baby-daddy. Sorry. I know you like that asshole."

"Thanks. But we're good, Jack and I."

"Why didn't you tell me about our old house and finding the receipt?"

"I didn't have anything concrete, and I didn't want to get your hopes up."

"I could've helped."

151

Carlotta gave him a pointed look. "It would've helped if you hadn't gotten arrested."

He wiped his hand over his mouth. "So you find the house where Mom is living, and you just walk up and ring the doorbell?"

"Pretty much. Our sister's name is Priscilla." She pulled another picture from her pocket.

It was half a strip of black and white photos from one of those booths. "She looks just like you. Is she a cool kid?"

"Yeah. Super smart, a little mature for her years."

"So tell me about Mom," he said. "Did she tell you why they left? Did they miss us?"

Tears pooled in Carlotta's eyes, setting off warning flags in his brain.

"What? Tell me."

"She has...memory problems."

"What do you mean?"

"She has dementia, Wes."

"You mean, like, Alzheimer's?"

She nodded, wiping at her eyes.

He didn't know he could feel anger and sadness and fear at the same time. "Does she remember us?"

"She does, but she gets the timelines confused. Sometimes she thinks I'm in high school, sometimes she thinks Priscilla is me."

"Does she know about Dad?"

"She thinks he's on a trip. And there are...some other things you should know."

"Like what?"

"Dad says he has evidence stashed that will exonerate him from the charges against him."

"What kind of evidence?"

"He didn't say. And if Valerie knows anything about it, she isn't saying, or can't recall."

Wes set back in his chair. "Stashed...like in a wall?"

She frowned. "What do you mean?"

"The counterfeit money—I found it inside a wall in the townhouse when I was doing repairs. I didn't tell anyone because I thought Dad had put it there for his use—and ours. I didn't know it was fake."

Carlotta gaped. "You found twenty-five thousand dollars in the wall and you didn't tell me?"

"It's more like, a half million."

Her eyes bugged. "What?"

"I was going to tell you."

"After you had a little fun?"

He shrugged. "It wasn't all fun. I paid off some bills."

"What bills?"

"My debts."

"You mean your loan shark?" Her hand flew to her mouth. "You paid off The Carver with counterfeit money?"

"Keep your voice down. I'm in deep shit. That's why I didn't want to get you involved. The Carver put a hit out on me."

"A hit?"

"Yeah, he sent a lug head named Leonard who works for his son Dillon to come here and take me out. That's why I can't leave."

"Leonard is dead."

Wes drew back. "Dead? How did that happen?"

"He walked out in front of a bus."

"No shit?"

"I saw it. I recognized him. I thought he was following *me*, that he was one of the bad guys trying to find Mom."

"Maybe since Leonard came to such a bad end, The Carver won't send someone else to take me out." Maybe they'd just wait until he got back to Atlanta and shoot him in the head then.

"I don't get it—can't you just tell The Carver you didn't know the money was fake and go back to owing him? Don't you work for him anyway?'

Wes frowned. "How do you know about that?"

Carlotta blanched. "That slipped out."

"Jack has a big mouth."

"So why can't you just go back to owing him?"

Wes had to find a nail to chew on to think about Chance's exact words the day he'd visited. "Actually, now that I think about it, Chance said it wasn't The Carver who was pissed at me, it was his son Dillon...he said I'd gotten him in a lot of trouble when I paid his dad with the counterfeit money."

"How would that get him in trouble with his father?"

The answer exploded into his head. "Because Dillon printed it? The Carver isn't a nice guy, but his business is on the up and up—if he thought Dillon was counterfeiting, he'd be furious."

"Because it would expose The Carver's entire operation to federal scrutiny."

Wes nodded.

Carlotta shook her head. "But why would money Dillon counterfeited be in the wall of the townhome?"

Wes's first thought was the time Mouse and his guys had come to install the security alarm—but the bag was in a part of the wall they didn't touch. Then he remembered something. "It was in a black plastic bag that had a design on it." He closed his eyes to think. "B...T...C, I think."

"Buckhead Tennis Club," Carlotta said. "It's where Dad played. In fact, I remember a conversation with a doctor who told me he was Dad's doubles partner. Dad told him someone in his firm was trying to frame him. He'd asked if he could bring something to him for safekeeping, but before it happened, Randolph had been arrested, then disappeared. I'll bet Randolph was planning to take him the bag of counterfeit money."

Wes scratched his head. "But how could counterfeit money be evidence that someone was trying to frame him?"

The answer slid into his head so quietly and so beautifully, it was almost poetic. And from the look on Carlotta's face, it had fallen into her head, too.

"Holy shit," he said.

"Those bastards—"

"—at Mashburn & Tully—"

"—were literally printing money." Carlotta steepled her hands over her nose.

"And I'll bet they were getting Dillon Carver to launder it for them," Wes said. "So when the money popped back into circulation, The Carver probably thought Dillon was up to his old tricks."

"So when Dad was accused of taking all that money," Carlotta said, "hundreds of millions of dollars..."

"He did take it," Wes said, "but it was fake!" He gave a whoop and a fist-pump. "Go, Dad!"

"Hey," the guard said, "keep it down. And you got ten minutes left."

"Oh, my gosh," Carlotta said. "Yesterday Mom said they had to leave because men were trying to kill them. At the time, it seemed fanciful, but now..."

"People would kill for a lot less," Wes said.

"I just remembered something else Mom said—that Dad was always bringing her these 'paper things' home from work."

"Paper things?"

"It's how she describes things when she can't remember the right words. I thought she meant books, but what if she meant paper money?"

"You think she knows where the rest of the counterfeit money is?"

"Could it be in our townhouse—in other walls?"

"No," Wes said. "I, uh, used a stud finder to cover every inch of the drywall and didn't find any more."

Carlotta massaged her temples. "I have to talk to Jack, and tell him everything."

"And I'm calling Liz, pronto. When we expose Mashburn &

Tully, the Secret Service isn't going to care about prosecuting me."

He might be out of jail in time to go on that date with Meg after all.

CHAPTER 23

CARLOTTA GLANCED at her watch to see exactly twenty seconds had passed since she'd last checked the time. She scanned the hotel lobby for Jack, but no dice.

"Come on," she muttered.

Granted, she'd interrupted him on a daytrip with Liz at Hoover Dam, and he'd shouted over the roar of the water it would take him a while to make excuses and get back, but Christ, she was about to burst. She considered texting him a headline to get him moving, but knowing Jack, if she sent something as outrageous as MASHBURN & TULLY ARE BIG FAT COUNTERFEITORS, he'd blow her off altogether. Instead, MEET ME ASAP HOTEL LOBBY would have to suffice.

After leaving the jail, buzzing with excitement over their sibling smarts, and reveling in how they were going to take down Mashburn & Tully, she realized what it might mean for Peter...and wondered if his growing agitation this week had anything to do with what was going on behind the scenes. The overheard conversations of him reporting back that neither she nor Wes had talked to Randolph made sense now—they didn't want him telling anyone what had happened.

Was someone at the firm also responsible for Randolph being jumped and stabbed in prison to try to silence him for good?

And what about the more troubling statements of time running out and needing to "pull the trigger"?

Her phone rang. Disappointment it wasn't Jack calling was replaced with concern when she saw Birch's name.

"Hello, Birch. Is everything okay?"

"Everything's fine. But I thought you'd want to know that Melanie has been talking up a storm since you left yesterday. She keeps repeating she's running out of room to store all the paper things Randolph brings her. Does that mean anything to you?"

"As a matter of fact, it does." She tried to tamp down her excitement. "Keep Mom talking as long as it doesn't upset her. I have an important meeting, but I'll be there as soon as I can."

"Will do."

She disconnected the call and scanned the lobby again. She didn't see Jack, but Hannah came around the corner, wearing her Goth garb. Carlotta waved and swore Hannah saw her, but her friend kept going. Perturbed, Carlotta ran her down.

"Hannah!"

When Hannah couldn't avoid her, she turned and feigned surprise. "Hey, how's it going? How's your dad?"

"He's maybe a tiny bit better, but it's hard to say."

"How's your mom?"

"That's always interesting. Remember I said she might know where the evidence is that would exonerate my dad? I think she's on the verge of revealing where she hid it. So even if the worst happens with Randolph, maybe it will still see the light of day."

Hannah was edging toward the elevator. "That's nice. Look, I have to be somewhere, so I'll catch you later." She bounded onto the elevator and the doors closed.

Carlotta scowled. What was going on with Hannah?

She released a frustrated groan. And where the heck was Jack?

CHAPTER 24

"YELLO?"

"Mouse, it's Wes."

"Jesus Louise Christ, why haven't you called me back? I left you a bunch of messages."

"Long story short, I didn't know the money I gave you was fake—really sorry about that. Then I got out to Vegas and spent a bunch more of the fake money, still not knowing it's fake. So I was arrested and my phones confiscated. Then I thought The Carver put a hit out on me, so I didn't want to get out of jail. Oh, and I guess you heard Leonard bought the farm? Anyway, I'm still in jail, but everything's going to work out and I'll be home soon."

"That was the short version?"

"I'm calling to tell you that the source of the counterfeit money is tied up with Dillon, so when the feds move in for the takedown, The Carver might be implicated by association. Cover yourself."

"Wow, thanks, Little Man. You might want to listen up, too. One of the messages you didn't get was about the person who hired the guy to stab your dad…"

CHAPTER 25

"A WOMAN?" Carlotta asked, squinting. "Are you sure he said a woman?"

"Yeah. Mouse said it was someone close to me and you, who has a lot of money. And not only did she hire someone to take out Dad, but she hired Leonard to follow you to find Mom, and take her out, too!"

"Alright, calm down, Wes. That doesn't make sense. What woman who's close to us and has a lot of money would care if Randolph—"

Then her heart stopped.

Hannah.

Her mind raced back through memories, stopping on pertinent factoids.

Finding out Hannah's family were clients of Randolph's and had lost almost everything.

Randolph Wren was the cause of a lot of grief in my world.

I was a little obsessed with finding out more about you.

Hannah had been the one with connections to the prison to get them inside…did she also have connections to arrange for the attack on Randolph?

Was there a connection between Hannah and Leonard? "Wes, did Chance know Leonard?"

"Yeah. They worked together sometimes. Why?"

Her head was spinning.

Hannah knew she was coming to Vegas to look for her mother, and had decided to come, too, at the last minute. How did she know Hannah had visited her family's hotel to have lunch with a prince?

How did she know HAL Properties even owned a hotel in Vegas?

"Sis, you still there?"

"Wes, I have to go. I'll call you later."

She disconnected the call and pulled up a search engine to find the HAL Properties company website. In the Find Locations box, she entered the state code for Nevada.

No results for NV.

But Hannah's family had regained their wealth. In fact, Hannah had concealed the fact that she was heir to the HAL Properties fortune because she didn't want to be associated with money. So why would she be fixed on revenge?

Still telling herself it couldn't be Hannah, she went back to the original search results page, and a link to an article jumped out at her. *Kathleen Kizer, Co-owner of HAL Properties, Commits Suicide.*

Carlotta covered her mouth with her hand.

Ha—I wish *my mother was an alcoholic.*

People check out, turn their backs on their families all the time.

"Not you, Hannah. Not you."

But even as she said the words, she remembered her friend and coworker Michael Lane, who had turned out to be a killer. And hadn't Jack's former partner Maria accused Carlotta of not knowing anything about her best friend?

Hannah had been acting so strange the past couple of days, moody and irritable.

So Coop gets an introduction to your new family, and I don't?

And oddly curious about her mother's mental capacity.

Your mother is awfully young for dementia, isn't she?

Did you ask your mother about the evidence your father said he had to exonerate him?

Hannah, who knew exactly where her mother was…and only a few minutes ago, Carlotta had said she thought her mother was on the verge of revealing where she'd hidden the evidence that could exonerate Randolph. And Hannah had rushed off…

She texted Hannah *Hey, where are you?*

AutoTextReply: Sorry, going to be out of reach for a while.

She'd never gotten an automatic response from Hannah before.

Carlotta's phone buzzed. It was a text from Jack.

Traffic is brutal…ETA to hotel 30 min.

She was trembling, wanted to call Jack and tell him what she suspected, but she didn't want him to go in with guns blazing. What if she was wrong? With a shaky hand she texted *Change of plans, mother in trouble, meet me there, will explain.*

CHAPTER 26

WHEN CARLOTTA DROVE up to the little ranch house, her heart dropped. A rental car sat in the driveway, like the model Hannah was driving.

She counted to ten to slow her galloping pulse. Hannah might've simply decided to drop by and introduce herself to Carlotta's new family, assuming they'd all be friends anyway when they returned to Atlanta.

After parking, she slipped up to the garage and peeked inside one of the small windows across the top. Birch's BMW was missing—he must be out running errands. She pulled out her phone to keep it handy in case she had to call for help.

"Drop it."

The voice made her blood run cold. Not Hannah.

Liz Fischer.

She would've bolted if not for the fact that her mother and Priscilla were probably in the house, defenseless. And Liz was holding a handgun to her head.

"Goddammit, Carlotta, drop the phone now."

She did. It landed with a crunch, signifying at least her screen was toast.

"Inside," Liz said. "Easy. I already saw one person's brains scattered all over the ground this week."

Carlotta turned the doorknob and pushed open the door. She walked inside carefully, scanning for her mother and Priscilla. They were in the kitchen, gagged and tied to chairs, their eyes wide and frightened. Carlotta pushed down a tide of anger—she wasn't going to be a hero...she just wanted them all to get out alive. She skimmed the room for exit strategies. There was one tall horizontal window over the sink—useless. And the back door, she recalled, was deadbolted shut—also useless.

Where are you, Jack?

"Actually," Liz said, "you might be able to help me, Carlotta."

"What do you want me to do, Liz?"

"Convince Valerie it's in everyone's best interests if she just tells me where the counterfeit bills are. She was talking nonsense before. The girl says she has dementia."

"That's right. What's your stake in all of this?"

"Every dime I have is invested in Mashburn & Tully. I'm not going to raise my child in poverty."

"Surely you don't think you're going to get away with this?"

"Surely I do. It's too bad about the girl, though. I didn't expect that little wrinkle. Although, I *could* take her with me and raise her myself. That would be better than the deal she has now."

Priscilla shot eye-daggers at Liz.

"Don't look at me like that," Liz said. "It's true. And you need to learn now you can't count on men. The dummy I paid to kill your daddy in prison—that didn't work. Randolph refuses to die. And the dummy I sent out here to follow Carlotta accidentally killed an FBI agent trying to get an address out of him, then he walked into a bus." She scoffed. "I have to do everything."

"Can I remove their gags?" Carlotta asked.

"Only Valerie's. No tricks."

As if she'd try anything clever with two of the most important people in her life in the room. She smiled at her mother. "Hi, Mom." As gently as she could, she untied the two knots in the strip of cloth.

"Do I know you?" Valerie said.

"Yes," Carlotta said. "We've met. I'm your daughter."

"Of course you are."

"Hurry," Liz barked. "Their gate-watcher will be back in an

hour."

Carlotta smoothed back Valerie's hair from her cheek. "Mom, have you seen any counterfeit money?"

"I don't think so."

"Liar," Liz yelled. "Where is it? Where's the three hundred million Randolph stole? There's only a half million in that dinky little townhouse in Atlanta. He had to put the rest of it in a warehouse somewhere. I want the key." She raised the gun and fired into the ceiling. The boom shattered the silence, and Valerie whimpered.

"Did that shake your memory loose, Valerie?"

Valerie glared at her. "I never liked you."

"But Randolph did. If you hadn't been such a pathetic drunk, he would've left you for me."

"Maybe that's why I got sick," Valerie mused. "So he would have to stay with me."

The profound statement gave Carlotta hope her mother was still in there somewhere.

"*Where* is the money?" Liz demanded.

Valerie looked off into space. "If these walls could talk, they might tell you, but I'm not going to."

Liz walked over and pushed the end of the gun into Valerie's hair. "Start talking now, crazy lady, or I'll blow away what little brain you have left."

Priscilla mumbled against her gag, trying to say something.

Liz nodded for Carlotta to remove it. As soon as the cloth was loose, Priscilla said, "It's in the walls, behind the paneling. Please don't hurt my mommy...or my sister."

Carlotta would have to thank the tike for that sentiment later. For now, Liz was pushing her toward a section of wainscoting.

"Tear it out," Liz said.

"With my bare hands?"

Liz sighed. "Stand back."

She shot into the paneling at the seam, and it gave way enough to reveal something was behind it. Another shot into the seam sent bits of paper flying into the air.

Liz laughed. "This is too perfect. A woman with dementia leaves on the stove, sets a fire, and burns the entire house down, with all that evidence inside. And a few victims."

She walked to the gas stove, turned on all the burners, and tossed a few kitchen towels on top to get a blaze going. Then she gave Carlotta a sad smile. "Sorry, Carlotta, but I don't have time to tie you up."

She lifted the gun and Carlotta closed her eyes. When the boom sounded, she thought getting shot in the face hadn't hurt as bad as she'd expected.

In fact, it hadn't hurt at all.

She opened her eyes gingerly to see Liz lying in a crumpled heap, a small dart in her neck.

"Birch!" Priscilla shouted, grinning down at the floor.

Birch lay with his head and one arm inside the doggie door, pointing a gun at Liz. "It's a tranquilizer," he said. "She'll be out for about thirty minutes."

Carlotta grabbed a knife and cut her mother's and Priscilla's bindings. "Take Mom out the front door," she yelled to Priscilla, coughing through the smoke. She tried to get close to the stove to turn off the burners, but the flames had caught the curtains and were spreading fast. She could hear Birch battering something against the back door, but the oxygen was quickly being sucked out of the room. After a deep breath in the crook of her elbow, she put her hands under Liz's shoulders and dragged her deadweight body down the hall and out the front door into the tumbled rock yard. Carlotta fell to her knees, wheezing and coughing.

At the sound of a car engine, she lifted her head to see Jack's rental barreling down the street. The brakes screeched, and he was out of the driver's seat before the vehicle stopped, his weapon drawn.

"No gun," Carlotta said, hacking up a lung. She pointed.

"Water hose. Help Birch." She crawled over to where Priscilla and Valerie were huddled and drew them into a group hug. "It's over. It's all over."

When she pulled back, her mother said, "Do I know you?"

"Yes. I'm your daughter, Carlotta."

"I like you," Valerie announced.

Carlotta blinked back tears. "I like you, too."

Birch came jogging out, his clothes scorched and his face soot-covered. "Everyone okay out here?"

"We're good," Prissy said. "You were awesome, Birch."

"Who *are* you?" Carlotta asked with a laugh.

"Someone Randolph knew he could trust," Birch said, hinting at a past. He knelt to examine Liz, checking her pulse.

A fire truck came screaming up the street, followed by an ambulance. Birch waved them up.

Jack came out and tossed down the garden hose. His hands and face were streaked with grime, and his clothes were wet. He stepped aside as the firemen bounded into the house, then made his way over to her.

"Are you okay?"

She nodded. "Liz...lost her way."

"A long time ago, from the sound of it. I'm sorry I didn't see it. How can you be so close to something and not recognize it for what it is?"

"Because we're human, Jack."

"Birch told me you pulled Liz out of there. Thank you, Carlotta, for saving her."

"I didn't do it for her, or for you," Carlotta said. "I did it for your child."

He leaned down and kissed her on the forehead. Then he walked with Liz's stretcher to the waiting ambulance. She was starting to come around. As Carlotta watched, Jack pulled out handcuffs, linked one around Liz's wrist and the other to the stretcher. His head and shoulders were bowed.

CHAPTER 27

"I CAN'T MARRY YOU, Peter. I'm sorry. Honestly, I shouldn't have said yes. I was caught up in the moment, and I think I was in love with the fantasy of us."

Carlotta slid the red Cartier ring box across the satiny bed covering toward where he sat. "I have to help my family heal, and I have to adjust to a new normal myself. It wouldn't be fair to either one of us if I tried to be there for them and be there for you, too. I hope you understand."

Peter's face creased with pain and sadness as he picked up the box. His eyes watered, and he bit into his lip to compose himself. "Of course I was expecting this. I'm going to have to get used to a new normal, too. I wouldn't want you to feel as if your life is on pause to see how all this shakes out." He exhaled noisily.

"You'll get through this, Peter. I'll still support you any way I can. All you have to do is ask."

A knock sounded at the door.

"Do you mind getting it?" Peter pulled out a handkerchief to wipe his face.

She pushed to her feet, walked across the opulent suite and opened the door.

Jack stood on the other side. "Hey."

"Is it over?"

He nodded. "The assets of Mashburn & Tully have been seized by the Justice Department, and the offices shuttered and padlocked."

"And the partners?"

"Warrants have been served on Ray Mashburn, James Brody, and Walt Tully. As soon as Tully's physically well enough, he'll be remanded to custody."

"Wow, how quickly things change."

"You can say that again." Jack straightened, then cleared his throat. "Listen, when the house here was torn apart to remove the counterfeit bills, we recovered an item I thought you might like."

"I can't imagine what it would be."

He picked up a shopping bag he'd set on the floor and pulled out a thick binder. "It's a photo album. I tried not to snoop, but from what I can tell, the first half are pictures of you and Wes your parents probably took with them. And the second half are pictures of Prissy growing up, with lots of other pictures of you and Wes worked in that seem a little odd."

"What do you mean?"

He opened the book and pointed to a picture of her. "They're more like surveillance pictures, as if you and Wes didn't know your picture was being taken."

The photo was of her in her mid-twenties, if she had to guess, based on the clothing. She was working behind the counter at Neiman's, handing a bag to a customer with a smile. Carlotta loosened the photo from the page and turned it over.

Carlotta, age 26, selling a top to Val

It was written in her father's handwriting. So she'd been waiting on her own mother and hadn't realized it.

"It looks as if they were keeping close tabs on you and Wes, even if it didn't feel like it."

Her heart surged. She closed the album and hugged it to her chest. "Thank you for this, Jack."

"Anything to see you smile," he said, his voice a little wistful. Then he nodded toward the door. "How's it going in there?"

"He's as ready as he'll ever be." She opened the door wider and Jack stepped inside.

Peter stood holding his briefcase and a carry-on bag. His suit was slightly rumpled and his face was shadowed. But he was standing up straight. He took a deep breath, then seemed to telegraph his preparedness to Jack.

Jack walked over to stand in front of him. "Peter Ashford, you're under arrest for conspiracy, racketeering, and fraud. You have the right to remain silent..."

Carlotta watched from across the room, giving Peter space and privacy. She hoped he would be able to shoulder the fallout as the case wound its way through the legal system. It would work against Peter that Walt Tully had confessed the entire scheme while he was recovering and Peter hadn't immediately gone to the authorities. But the fact that he had worked with Walt to try to mitigate the losses for some clients who were living on fixed incomes would hold some sway.

When Jack had finished reciting the Miranda rights, he cuffed Peter's hands in front of him and draped his jacket over the metal so it wasn't obvious he was being criminally escorted back to Atlanta. Jack handed Peter his briefcase, then picked up the carry-on. Carlotta appreciated Jack's tact in the awkward encounter—the two men hadn't always seen eye to eye. As they left together, Peter gave her a brave smile, and she nodded in reassurance.

The door had nearly closed when Jack stuck his head and shoulders back in. "I almost forgot. There's one more thing the feds thought you might appreciate, so they flew it in on a government jet."

Carlotta was intrigued. "What is it?"

Jack opened the door wider to reveal her father. Randolph Wren was bandaged and on a cane, but standing. And smiling.

"Hi, sweetheart."

Her emotions overflowed. She didn't have words to express how it felt to see him free and his name cleared. She hugged him gingerly in deference to his injuries, then pulled back and studied his face. "I can't believe you're here."

When they gave me the chance to come and see you and Wes,

and Val and Prissy before we pick up and move to Atlanta, I had to do it. And they took good care of me. I'm just sore."

"Sit down," she said, leading him to a comfortable chair. "I'll get us something to drink."

When she came back to sit near him, they both looked at each other for the longest time, then laughed and clasped hands. Her father's voice was strong, and his face still handsome, with just a few more lines than she remembered.

"The other reason I wanted to come," Randolph said, "is because I didn't want to wait one day longer to give you an explanation for what happened. Of course, I'll tell Wesley whatever he wants to know, but I wanted this time with you, because I feel as if I owe you the most for everything you've done for our family."

Carlotta smiled through her tears. "I don't know if I deserve that praise, but I'd be lying if I said I didn't want answers to questions I've wondered about for so long."

"Well, now that you know what was going on at the firm, you probably understand how much money and power was at stake. I didn't know about the counterfeiting—they needed someone with clean accounts to keep up appearances."

"How did you find out what was going on?"

He gave a little laugh. "By accident. I was walking through the office one night after closing, and saw a hundred-dollar bill on the floor. I put it in my wallet and forgot about it, and a few days later, I was having lunch with a banker friend. I started to pay with the hundred and he noticed something strange about it. But when he ran it through all his tests, it came back as a real hundred. He said it was actually printed on currency paper, and was the best fake money he'd ever seen. He used it to develop more sophisticated anti-fraud testing."

"So you confronted the partners?"

"I did, because I assumed they didn't know what was going on, that it was some junior broker or intern using our facilities at night. We found the operation in a hidden room. What I didn't know and still can't believe is Walt and Brody were the masterminds. When I told them I was going to the feds, they played along, when really, they were working behind the scenes to make me the scapegoat. When I realized what was happening, I started smuggling the bills out, a few at a time."

"There wasn't anyone in the Justice Department you could go to?"

"I went to the FBI and asked for protection. But when Valerie and I went to meet them, we were ambushed and shot at. Knowing what I know now, I think it was someone in Dillon Carver's crime organization, at the behest of either someone at the firm or at the FBI. We didn't know who to trust. Val told me she was pregnant and wanted to get sober. I didn't want to leave her for you to deal with on top of Wes, and God knows that was more responsibility than was fair."

Her father paused for a drink of water, clearly lost in the memories. "We left town thinking we'd give the FBI time to arrange something. We had every intention of coming back. But then the baby was born, and Val was having more and more emotional issues. I got the opportunity to take over a dead man's identity—Bill Rudolph. I thought it was close enough to Randolph that no one would notice I said one thing and spelled it another way. I got a job as a dealer in a casino in Vegas, and started day trading. Things were…not bad. We were actually thinking about turning ourselves in so we could be with you and Wes, even if we all had to go into witness protection.

He sighed. "But then Val's mind started slipping, and I knew if we all got together, you'd be shouldering the burden of Wes and your mom and your baby sister. Even if we hired people, to help, I knew emotionally it would be too much. So…we stayed away."

"Until you saved my life," Carlotta said.

"I'd bought our former house in Buckhead a few months prior, and because I trusted Birch, I was making more trips to fix up the house and I could monitor you and Wes enough to know what your lives were like. I think I had fantasies that if we could all just move back into that house, we'd have our old lives back. It was pure happenstance I was there the day you were attacked. I didn't think about getting caught, I just ran over there."

She squeezed his hand. "I'm happy you did."

"So am I. I have no regrets. Especially since it started the ball rolling on the original case. My mistake was I didn't know how involved Liz was in the counterfeiting. They were still doing it, but they'd gotten much better at it." He gave her a little smile. "For what it's worth, I don't think Peter knew what was going on. He might've suspected, but I doubt they find his fingerprints on anything."

She smiled. "Thank you. I'm very fond of Peter."

A knock sounded at the door. Carlotta went to open it and cried out when she saw Wes on the other side.

"Can you believe what we did?" He hugged her tight and danced around. "We took Mashburn & Tully *down*."

"You sure did."

Wes's head came up and he froze.

"Hi, son."

Wes ran to Randolph like a ten-year-old boy, and from the way he held on, Carlotta decided he might never let go.

CHAPTER 28

"I'M HERE TO EAT CROW," Hannah said. "Not literally, although I did eat a pigeon once and it wasn't terrible."

Carlotta squinted at her friend. "What?"

"Never mind. The point is, I might have been a little hard on Peter. And it's not because I feel sorry for him that you dumped him and he's going to jail. It's because he contacted my parents earlier this week and told them to withdraw any investments they still had with Mashburn & Tully. He knew things were going south, and he didn't want them to lose money again. I think that was a stand-up thing to do."

"Thank you for sharing," Carlotta said. "Um, speaking of your parents."

Hannah's eyebrows shot up. "What about them?"

Carlotta sighed. "Hannah, I wasn't snooping. Okay—I was snooping. I came across an article that mentioned your mother committed suicide."

"Right," Hannah said.

"I just think it's bizarre that you've never mentioned it."

"I wasn't close to my mother. My stepmother raised me. So when I say parents, I mean my dad and my stepmom."

"But the article said she was a co-owner of HAL Properties."

"Right. My dad started the business, and when they split up, he gave her some ownership in it because I think he was afraid it would be the only steady income she'd have."

"Oh. That...makes sense."

"So there is something else," Hannah said. "I know I've been acting a little shitty the past few days. I was keeping something from you, and I want to come clean before I head back to Atlanta."

"I'm on pins and needles," Carlotta said. "What?"

Hannah winced and held out her beringed left hand. "Chance and I got married!"

CHAPTER 29

"I CAN'T THANK YOU ENOUGH for doing this," Carlotta said over the aisle to Coop.

He shrugged. "Staying a couple extra days in Vegas to fly back with you and Valerie and Prissy and Birch? That's no hardship."

"It's an inconvenience," she said. "But it makes me more calm to know you're close by if we need you."

"That's a given," Coop said. "No matter where you are."

She smiled. "You've been good to me and to Wes."

"Really happy to hear all those charges were dropped and Wes is back in Atlanta."

"I think he and Dad have been having fun fixing up the house before Mom and Prissy get there."

"Is Birch okay with relocating?"

"I guess so." Then she squinted. "There's a story there."

"Are you and Wes going to live in the Buckhead house, too?"

"I'm sure we'll be there a lot, but we're going to stay in the townhouse, maybe fix it up."

"Any chance you'll have time to help me with some body moving jobs?"

"Call me. And you know Hannah's always up for a dead body."

"Wow, I can't believe she's married."

Carlotta laughed. "I guess she got tired of waiting for you."

"Hm," Coop said with a little smile. "Maybe I'm waiting for someone, too."

The flight attendant announcement to fasten seatbelts saved Carlotta from responding. She turned to help her mother with her belt.

"Did you bring a paper thing?" Valerie asked, nodding to the binder on Carlotta's lap.

"It's like a book. It's a family photo album. I thought maybe we could look at it during our trip home to Atlanta."

"I'd like that," her mother said. "What is your name again?"

"Carlotta."

"Right. And you're my daughter."

"That's right." Carlotta remembered something and pulled out her phone. "Mom, do you remember writing this on a wall in a coffee shop bathroom?"

"No. What is it?"

"That's your name. Valerie W. You wrote it one day when you were in there, and then I saw it. That's how I knew you were close by."

"Valerie knew you'd come looking for me," her mother said.

Carlotta squeezed her hand.

"Young lady?"

"Yes, Mom?"

"That nice friend of yours over there with the stethoscope. Is his name Cooper Craft?"

Carlotta glanced across the plane aisle at Coop, and her heart expanded with affection. She looked back to her mom. "Yes, that's right."

Valerie pointed to the picture Carlotta had shown her. "Why is his name written on the wall above mine?"

-The End-

A NOTE FROM THE AUTHOR

Thank you so very much for reading 8 BODIES IS ENOUGH! I hope you enjoyed this book as much as I enjoyed writing it. No matter how many projects take me away from Body Movers, I'm always happy to come back to these characters I know and love. Please know I'll be writing more Body Movers books—Carlotta and the gang still have lots of adventures to go on! But I wanted to tie up a lot of loose ends in this book so the characters could start in a fresh place in book 9.

If you enjoyed 8 BODIES IS ENOUGH and feel inclined to leave a review at your favorite online bookseller, I would appreciate it very much. Reviews help my books find new readers, which means I can keep writing new stories! Plus I always want to know what my readers are thinking. Thank you for your support— without readers like you, there wouldn't be a Body Movers series!

Are you signed up to receive notices of my future book releases? If not, please visit www.stephaniebond.com and enter your email address. I promise not to flood you with emails and I will never share or sell your address. And you can unsubscribe at any time. While you're on my website, check out the FAQs page for more information about the history (and future) of the Body Mover series.

Thanks again for your time and interest, and for telling your friends about my books. As long as you keep reading, I'll keep writing!

Happy reading!

Stephanie Bond

OTHER WORKS BY STEPHANIE BOND

Humorous romantic mysteries:
COMA GIRL—*You can learn a lot when people think you aren't listening.*
TWO GUYS DETECTIVE AGENCY—*Even Victoria can't keep a secret from us...*
OUR HUSBAND—*Hell hath no fury like three women scorned!*
KILL THE COMPETITION—*There's only one sure way to the top...*
I THINK I LOVE YOU—*Sisters share everything in their closets...including the skeletons.*
GOT YOUR NUMBER—*You can run, but your past will eventually catch up with you.*
WHOLE LOTTA TROUBLE—*They didn't plan on getting caught...*
IN DEEP VOODOO—*A woman stabs a voodoo doll of her ex, and then he's found murdered!*
VOODOO OR DIE—*Another voodoo doll, another untimely demise...*
BUMP IN THE NIGHT—*a short mystery*

***Body Movers* series:**
PARTY CRASHERS (full-length prequel)
BODY MOVERS
2 BODIES FOR THE PRICE OF 1
3 MEN AND A BODY
4 BODIES AND A FUNERAL
5 BODIES TO DIE FOR
6 KILLER BODIES
6 ½ BODY PARTS (novella)
7 BRIDES FOR SEVEN BODIES
8 BODIES IS ENOUGH

Romances:

ALMOST A FAMILY—*Fate gave them a second chance at love...*

LICENSE TO THRILL—*She's between a rock and a hard body...*

STOP THE WEDDING!—*If anyone objects to this wedding, speak now...*

THREE WISHES—*Be careful what you wish for!*

The Southern Roads series:

BABY, I'M YOURS (novella)

BABY, DRIVE SOUTH

BABY, COME HOME

BABY, DON'T GO

BABY, I'M BACK (novella)

BABY, HOLD ON (novella)

BABY, IT'S YOU (novella)

Nonfiction:

GET A LIFE! 8 STEPS TO CREATE YOUR OWN LIFE LIST—*a short how-to for mapping out your personal life list!*

YOUR PERSONAL FICTION-WRITING COACH: *365 Days of Motivation & Tips to Write a Great Book!*

ABOUT THE AUTHOR

Stephanie Bond was seven years deep into a corporate career in computer programming and pursuing an MBA at night when an instructor remarked she had a flair for writing and suggested she submit material to academic journals. But Stephanie was more interested in writing fiction—more specifically, romance and mystery novels. After writing in her spare time for two years, she sold her first manuscript; after selling ten additional projects to two publishers, she left her corporate job to write fiction full-time. To-date, Stephanie has more than seventy published novels to her name, including the popular BODY MOVERS humorous mystery series, and STOP THE WEDDING!, a romantic comedy adapted into a movie for the Hallmark Channel. Stephanie lives in Atlanta, where she is probably working on a story at this very moment. For more information on Stephanie's books, visit www.stephaniebond.com.

COPYRIGHT INFORMATION